SEPTUM

A DEEPER THAN HELL PARAQUEL

JOSHUA MILLICAN

Cover Design by Christian Francis.

Author Photo by Ama Lee.

Encyclopocalypse Publications
www.encyclopocalypse.com

This one's for you, Hunny Bunny. Your power amazes me!

-JM

Author's Note

Technically, *Septum* is *Deeper Than Hell Part 2*. But it's not a conventional sequel or prequel. *Septum* is a **paraquel**: A story that takes place simultaneously with or in parallel to another story. There is actually very little direct overlap between *Septum* and *Deeper Than Hell*. While having read *Deeper Than Hell* will certainly give you an expanded understanding of this particular fictional universe, it is not strictly necessary to be familiar with that text in order to connect with this one.

Go on, dive in!

Prologue

I'd been "taken in", to put it non-confrontationally, by Meister Hauptnadel (whose name I can't even write without wincing), an egomaniacal German psychonaut who sounded like your stereotypical mad scientist. He presides over a community called The Acolytes of Ascension...

He eventually introduced me to Sybil, an Acolyte with her eyes and mouth sewn shut. Her nose was grossly distended into a single, gaping nostril that emitted a slurping noise with every inhalation, a farting noise with each exhalation. Hauptnadel dragged her around by a thick black braid extending from the top of her head.

"Sybil iss psychic," the madman told me. "Vonce vee took her eyes und her tongue, she learnt to decipher riddles und premonitions by zee sense off schmell exclusifely."

Hauptnadel removed the plug in her forehead, injected her brain with a finger-syringe, and inserted a glass globe to collect the sloshing fluids. "She eats trough her nose, she fucks trough her nose..." he told me, thrusting his hips to emphasize the F-word. He pulled her onto my torture table. "...Vhich is vie I hat to remoof her scheptum."

Sybil, whose ears were intact, nodded and snorted in agreement. He pulled the sheet away from my emaciated body.

"Now let's see vhat she can tell me about you!"

He shoved Sybil's head between my legs where she feverishly sniffed my testicles, like a pig rooting around for a truffle. After a few moments, she reached out to Hauptnadel, who handed her some chalk and a piece of slate. "Oh, zis iss not goot," he bemoaned as he revealed Sybil's scrawl:

"He's a coward!"

— Sonny Demarco - *Deeper Than Hell*

Sybil the Hellraiser

Don't look at me like that, with your pity. I'll be pleased to shock you, pleased to disturb you, pleased to cause a visceral physical reaction within you. Your horror nourishes me. But your pity makes me want to vomit.

You think you know me? Described by a castaway I merely crossed paths with as he spiraled into Hell? He looked at me with horror and disgust. He saw an abomination. But I opened my mind to him. I inhaled him. And even though my eyes are sewn shut, I saw his soul. I explored his cowardly constitution. I used my abilities to see his past and his present—his truth. He was Hellbound. I, on the other hand, was in the midst of a great Ascension. So, who do you want to believe?

You want to know if it's true. You want to know if I fuck with my nose. You're obsessed with the idea. It was crass for my Earthly Master to put it in such basic terms, but not completely inaccurate. Yes, my mouth is sewn shut, but the removal of my septum (plus my six top-front teeth and gums, and the front half of my hard pallet) allows for access to the mucus membranes in my cheeks. My tongue is intact and can be pushed through my mono-nostril. I can offer a somewhat unique rendition of fellatio or cunnilingus. For me, these occasions are both sensual and spiritual.

If you imagined me a rag-doll skull-fuck know this: I have two metal quills embedded in my tongue. Mostly, they lay flat and pointed backwards towards my throat in a safe position. But a lever under my tongue, engaged by my bottom front teeth, snaps them up and outward, fangs that can pierce and slice with surgical precision. Nothing enters my skull without permission.

My Earthly Master enters my skull through the hole in my forehead, pierces my brain with his needle fingers, injects the sweet serums that makes my soul sing.

But if you had asked me, I'd say, "No. I experience the world through my nose. But I fuck with my pussy." That, in case you were wondering, is not sewn shut and never will be probably.

If that's all you really wanted to know, then away with you. Take your pity and shove it. The rest of you, if you think you can handle it, I have much more to tell. Things more interesting and much more horrifying than my nose.

I wear a clit cap. What's that? Imagine a surgical steel robin's egg, even smaller. Now bisect it top to bottom and hollow it out. It rests comfortably in the fold at the crest of my labia majora, encapsulating my hood and the pearl within its hollow. Initially, it's held in place with your standard Christina piercing. Also known as a Venus piercing, it embeds a curved barbell above the labial convergence, below the pubic mound. It's not a particularly popular procedure above ground as it doesn't enhance sexual gratification per se. But that's apropos in my case. Still, if this were the clip cap's only area of connection it would be useless, spinning like the cover of a peephole when the point is to keep it shut tight.

While the method of installation varies among those in the congregation adorned with clit caps, mine is held firmly in place by four delicate yet unbreakable tungsten chains and four barbed hooks. Imagine the clip cap is a torso and the Christina pierces the head. The first two chains extend upwards like arms, anchored to hooks in my upper pelvis that pierce not only my skin and muscle, but each of my ovaries internally. In addition to the constant throb of pulling and healing flesh, these increase the pains of menstruation exponentially, exquisitely.

The bottom two chains extend from the egg like legs and run around back in the creases between my entire pussy and upper-inner thigh. They wrap around my legs several times beneath the curve of my ass before finally connecting to hooks in the meat of my buttocks. As my weight fluctuates with hormones, trauma, and cosmic pulls, the chains are often taut, carving canyons in my skin. Exquisite. The loose ends of chains are assembled and woven around my hips, creating a look not dissimilar to a garter belt, though completely unintentional. They're cinched by a lock that hangs painfully over my navel.

It's not a chastity belt. My clit cap does not interfere with any of my natural functions, ablutions, or the execution of my carnal desires. But it does hamper, yes. It does inhibit. It's a dampener. It creates a desperate longing. And by depriving myself of this satisfaction, I forge a spiritual path. Because pain, even submission, isn't solely about suffering. That's only half of the equations. Prolonged and endured, suffering becomes a source of power. My body is not a prisoner and my Earthly Master doesn't hold the key. I do. The key, quite literally, has been sterilized and surgically implanted near the back of my neck. I need only claw it out to unlock myself.

I still come. I come and I shudder and I howl and I gush. As any gynecological physiologist can explain, the clitoris is much more than just the exposed nub. It has tendrils descending into and encircle the entire canal, making any distinction between clitoral and vaginal orgasms technically irrelevant. It's amazing how little some women understand about our own bodies. Yes, I come. The vibrations of an artificial phallus can be an immediate trigger. But it's not the same. I come, and I come often. But I don't come like I used to.

I swell and I strain until my throbbing hot ruby is shrieking for the human touch, the ultimate ignition. It pulsates, it morphs, it seeks to extricate its tentacles, to rebel against its cage, to free the suffocating rosebud. It becomes a monster, gnashing at its constraints, threatening to pull free from the chains and the very body that contains it. And still, it's denied that moment of extreme, blissful obliteration. And so the want grows until the need is genuine, intensified, magnified, sanctified.

To what end? No, perpetual denial is not its own reward. As a rider of The Great Pendulum, I understand the balanced dogma of extremity. Nature abhors and vacuum and cherishes symmetry. When I do unlock my chains to release the deprived and starving detainee, I expect a glorious explosion. A butterfly will beat its wings in Africa or an astronaut will whisper something nasty on the ISS, and these near-undetectable vibrations will be enough to start a chain reaction destine to redefine the universally accepted parameters of an orgasm. A feedback loop encapsulating The Big Bang until the end of the Universe in a fraction of a second, again and again into forever. I imagine being turned inside-out at the yoni, reassembled into a statue of an alien flower carved out of flesh and bone. My vital organs and entrails adorning the gruesome splendor. Radiating orbs of energy. Shredding the very fabric of this tantric planet. The warmest oblivion.

Obviously, I'm speaking in metaphors. Still, there's a real possibility that this first unbridled release will be fatal. It's a risk I'm willing to take. And the principals and expectations associated with my clit cap are at the root of all of my modifications. I endure the depraved depths of my descent so that, one day, I may bask in the most resplendent of illuminations. White light and angels singing until, inevitably, The Great Pendulum snaps me back down again. And again.

Of course I'm obsessive with *Hellraiser*. I imagine we all are, the Acolytes. But expect consequences for articulating as much. A new recruit, a potential cadet, affectionately referred to my Earthly Master as "Papa Pinhead". He was summarily drugged within an inch of his life, branded with an insignia designating rejection, and, days later, unceremoniously dumped outside Sunset Hospital Emergency on South Maryland Parkway. Returning him to the surface was an exceptionally complicated process, as you will come to understand, but illustrates the disdain my Earthly Master has for comparisons. Still, the objective truth is, if our organization was a religion and The Great Pendulum was our God, then Clive Barker would be Jesus Christ. A true interdimensional emissary.

But we're not a religion. And while Barker may have given us an unspoken vocabulary to understand our desires, our identities, we are unique unto ourselves. A stated affiliation with or obvious affinity for Barker would potentially push our organization into the realms of fiction. We are not fiction. You won't find our stories in the Horror aisle of your local bookstore. We are not imitators. Yes, my Earthly Master desires to become something more than human, something akin to an immortal angel/demon hybrid. And yes, I seek to aid him in his endeavors, be they valid or misguided. Because we all desire to be something more than human. It is this desire that brought most of us underground, like moths to a flame. We seek to venture past the bounds of physical and psychological extremities. Beyond the flesh, bones, and viscera that comprise us. The realms we seek to explore are inner-space and interdimensional. Foreboding sanctums beyond infinite horizons and dark universes under the stairs or just behind the walls. We wander the Labyrinth. We are, by definition, Cenobites. But we are not Cenobites. We are Acolytes.

I've been obsessed with *Hellraiser* since someone recommended it to me during my first year at Sacramento City

College. I brought a TV and DVD player into my room so I could watch it alone, in the dark, in my bed. Repeatedly. At least ninety-nine times over the course of a single semester. And even though these characters made only brief appearances in Barker's first cinematic endeavor, I was obsessed with the Cenobites. I didn't want to meet them like Frank Cotton—I wanted to be them. Pinhead: Stately, controlled, frayed chaos intertwined with surgical precision. Butterball: Bloated with sin, proudly grotesque, wise, wicked, somehow sublime. Chatterer made me wet, wearing his scar tissue like a gimp's mask. A powerful enforcer but also a rule-breaker. His clicking teeth transmitting harrowing poetry. Female: Of course she's the one I adored the most. Fiercely brave yet undeniably forlorn, an entity capable of both dispensing and suffering ruthless abuses. A true switch.

They were a family, and I was overjoyed to reunite when I naturally began my study of *Hellbound: Hellraiser II*. Pinhead and Butterball displayed subtle changes, but Chatterer and Female were noticeably renovated. The enforcer now had eyes, a reward for good behavior as a faithful lieutenant, no doubt. Female was completely transformed, quite literally. The character was played by Grace Kirby in 1987's *Hellraiser* and replaced by Barbie Wilde in 1989's *Hellbound*. This incongruity, however, bothered me not a bit. I saw it as indicative of Female's continued evolution.

The remnants of wispy hair that made Female pitiable in *Hellraiser* were gone, and her smooth head conveyed power. Her sunken eyes were pushing forward, as though awakened from a sleep deeper than death. She had not only endured her transformation but exceeded in adaptation, earning her role as The Hell Priest's right hand Priestess. Her Grecian beauty, a prize for unwavering dedication to Leviathan's credos. A prize and a punishment.

Still, I've always had a soft spot for Kirby's portrayal and aesthetic. As a work in progress myself, there's more of an innate kinship. And I've often found myself wondering, "What ever became of Kirby?" Who was she? IMDB informed me that she's Clive Barker's cousin, so maybe she took the role as a favor. She was already an established actress. Why, then, was *Hellraiser* her final cinematic endeavor? Had she been touched by the darkness of the sets, the cruelty of her character, or the implications of punishment beyond pain? Was she too scared to return for the sequel, panicking at the mere thought donning the latex and leather accoutrements?

Did you know that before the character was simply dubbed Female she was called Deep Throat? Her appliance holds open a vertical slit cut through her windpipe. The wound looks vaginal. That, combined with the pornographic moniker makes the implication clear: She has sex with her throat. She gets fucked in the neck. Barbie Wilde confirmed as much in *Hellbound Hearts* (a collection of stories inspired by *The Hellbound Heart*). When the Cenobite Grillard completed the transformation of Sister Nikoletta, he "used" each of her holes before thrusting her into the Labyrinth.

Of course I read *The Hellbound Heart*. Of course it thrilled me to discover that Pinhead was not the leader, rather an androgynous, girlish attendant. The real leader of the Cenobites is female, scarred and beautiful, a convergence of keloids crisscrossing her pubic mound. I learned more about Cenobite genealogy and The Order of the Gash. But rather than attempting to reconcile the differences between the *Hellraiser* franchise and the novella that spawned it, I compartmentalize, appreciating them both for their own merits without attempting to mold the two into one. To that end, I must admit that the first time I saw the original band of Cenobites destroyed by insidious Dr. Philip Channard (played by Kenneth Cranham), I slammed the door and screamed so hard my roommate called the cops.

Of course I explored the entirety of *Hellraiser*'s cinematic universe. *Hellraiser III: Hell On Earth* made me wonder if places like The Boiler Room actually existed, spurning me to investigate Goth clubs and, eventually, BDSM. I welcomed the re-manifestation of Pinhead and the introduction of Elliot Spenser. I love Doug Bradley. And I welcomed the addition of new Cenobites though I was disappointed by Dreamer. A female Cenobite who tortured her victims with cigarettes? Come now. Respectfully, Mr. Peter Atkins, you could have done better than that.

Of course I loved *Hellraiser IV: Bloodline* for its scope and bravery. Of course I loved Angelique, the first truly worthy successor to the Original Female Cenobite. But I'm also objective enough to admit that the straight-to-DVD era of the *Hellraiser* franchise has been, to put it kindly, uneven. The low point came when Pinhead wielded a cleaver in *Hellworld*. The audacity! The very idea of the entity able to summon hooks and chains out of ether using a device as primitive as a cleaver is almost sacrilegious. I didn't mind that Pinhead was "fat" in *Revelations*, as that installment was at least a true *Hellraiser* sequel and, at best, an accurate extension of Barker's original themes (though he has famously claimed otherwise). I loved the inventiveness of *Judgment*. And I understand that, since my relocation underground, a new *Hellraiser* has been released on a streaming platform. While I'm thrilled to hear that it features a female Pinhead and support any continuation of Barker's legacy, I doubt I'll ever see it. I doubt I'll ever look at another television, even if I cut my eyelids open again.

As much as I love him, I actually don't mind when Pinhead is portrayed by actors other than Doug Bradley. As the graphic novels from BOOM! Studios explain, the nails are not unique to Elliot Spenser. The grid and nails are, in fact, a designation of rank. Priests come and go, even when they're immortal. Change is inevitable.

Likewise as much as I adore Nicholas Vince as The

Chatterer I also love the various Pseudo-Chatterer manifestations (the dogs, the torso, the female) who have dotted the franchise. The clicking of teeth is a warning: You are in the presence of a predator—something that can never be tamed.

But most of all, I love The Wire Twins from Scott Derrickson's criminally underrated *Hellraiser V: Inferno*. These are the entities who, in my opinion, most accurately represent Cenobites as described in *The Hellbound Heart*. Scarred and carved, sexually ferocious, the most welcoming and devastating of sirens. Their sense of touch and stimulation no doubt enhanced since sacrificing their eyes, The Wire Twins concoct psychedelic perversions like witches around a cauldron.

Did Deep Throat, The Wire Twins, and other Cenobites inspire my own appliances, my modifications and my transformation? I'd be lying to claim otherwise. But you could probably trace the explosion in popularity of all body modifications to the release of *Hellraiser*. Punk rock started it, but Barker made the practice transgressive and transcendent. Ears, even those cluttered with studs and hoops, quickly became passé unless their lobes were stretched. That's why I abandoned earrings like so much useless glitter. I walked into a tattoo and piercing parlor on 30th street without an appointment on my 19th birthday. I asked for the biggest, heaviest ring my septum could support. I could smell the dried blood and healing cartilage for weeks afterwards. It was the sweetest perfume.

My initial foray into the Goth scene, my search for a real-life Boiler Room or a tribe of actual Cenobites, met with mixed results. For starters, I don't think Goth culture as it existed in the 1980s and 1990s is still alive in the 21st Century. It's evolved into something else—something expansive, yes, but also diluted. In Sacramento, I attended gatherings at Clardeon, District 30, Badlands, Sidetrax, and Faces Nightclub. I attended Coven, Necromancy, Club Absolution, and a dozen others. I widened my search radius into San Francisco, finding the DNA Lounge,

The Cat Club, Bondage A-Go-Go, Raven Bar, Strangelove, Tera Nova, and even The Edwardian Ball, and on and on...

But none of these venues or events scratched my particular itch, in spite of the fact that Goth is a broad umbrella with numerous side-streets and avenues. I liked certain aspects of the scene and hated others. Loved Rammstein, Mushroomhead, and Nine Inch Nails. Hated Morrissey, Joy Division, and Marilyn Manson. Loved The Cure. Hated Korn. Loved black hair and inspired body art. Hated neon hair and Hot Topic. Loved the rampant pansexuality. Hated all the boys trying to look like The Crow. Loved the Wicca. Hated the vampires. Loved the promise of potential dangers and deviant pleasures. Hated just about everyone I met. Even the most committed enthusiasts seemed somehow phony, temporary, transient. I didn't want to be a weekend warrior, a cosplayer, a poser. I didn't want to play dress-up and I didn't want to get fucked up. I wanted to be transformed and I wanted to be obliterated. I wanted to be cast into Hell. I wanted to be a Cenobite.

It was years before I understood why those efforts had been in vain and found the missing ingredient I needed to make the connections I desperately wanted. Drugs. While never officially Straight-Edge, I scoffed at the popularity of drugs as a teen and young adulthood. It's easy to have disdain for something that you can't have, masking resentment with criticisms lobbed at those who appreciated imbibement. I rolled my eyes at every drunk frat boy or stoner boy who attempted to snag my attention. Yes, I started drinking once I turned 21, but all that ever got me was dehydration hangovers and a string of bad one-night stands.

I didn't realize how badly I needed drugs. Not merely to endure the mendacity of bastardized Goth culture, but in order to see beyond The Matrix, in order to interpret signs leading to forbidden portals and the hints of worlds beyond. Not all drugs, of course. Cocaine, Adderall, methamphetamines: These will help you dance and fuck all night but won't move the needle in terms of spiritual or metaphysical desires. Opioids are useless beyond pain relief, never inspiring or propagating truly creative ambitions. Alcohol is taxing. Cannabis is perfect for what it is, and it is extraordinary, but it's rarely powerful enough for interdimensional manifestations. Not in its natural state, anyway.

Once discovered, drugs of the hallucinogenic variety became my mainstay. Psilocybin, mescaline, peyote, nitrous oxide, ecstasy, PCP, DMT, and random research chemicals imported from China. Anything that got me in touch with sacred geometry. My drug of choice, you may have guessed, is LSD. LSD became a close friend, a near-constant confidant. When my world went to Hell, LSD became my consummate companion.

I met Byron at an outdoor electronica festival on Treasure Island in the San Francisco Bay. As I walked past him, he threw a mushroom at my head. I stopped and looked at him with suspicious eyes. I looked down at the mushroom and then back at Byron with a smile. "Got any more of those?" I asked. Byron reached into his back-pack and pulled out an entire pound. Byron wasn't a drug dealer. Even better. Byron was a trust fund kid who never went out without a full dispensary of illegal intoxicants. He loved being "that guy" as in, "that guy who's always giving away free drugs." Byron shared happily and indiscriminately. Men, women, boys, and girls. Friends, acquaintances, strangers, and enemies.

Even before we met, I'd seen him on the scene. Byron must have gone out even more than I did. Byron wasn't a true Goth. It wasn't the music or the aesthetic that brought him to our gatherings. It was the people. Byron loved people. He loved Burning Man and Bonnaroo and Lollapalooza. He loved private parties at the Presidio and dive-bar gatherings with equal affection. He could be the life of the party. But he had a dark side. As generous as Byron was with his many stashes, no one did more drugs than he did. Not in the Bay Area, anyway.

When I saw him again outside The Cat Club a few weeks later, something had changed. He was in a state. Nervous, chain smoking, even chocking back waves of nausea. I gave him the silent "What's up?" head nod, but he just shook his head. He was mumbling something I couldn't quite hear, so I approached.

"What did you say?"

"Are you real?" he asked me, calm at first before repeating himself in frantic triplicate. "Are you real? Are you real? Are you real?"

"Too much ketamine tonight?" I asked with a smile, hoping to lighten the mood. Byron smiled for a split second before re-agitating.

"I think I'm glitching out," he confessed, but articulating his paranoia seemed only to amplify it.

"Why are you freaking out?" I asked, extending an arm to give his shoulder a comforting squeeze.

"I'm not 'freaking out'. I'm glitching out!" he clarified with dread and annoyance.

"What does that even mean?"

"Do you play video games?" he countered.

"Sometimes," I admitted.

"Have you ever gotten stuck behind a wall?"

I shrugged and shook my head having no idea, at first, what he was talking about. For a split second I imagined that classic *Twilight Zone* episode, "Little Girl Lost".

"Do you remember the Loma Prieta earthquake? 1989? Interrupted the World Series? Freeways collapsed?"

I thought he was changing the subject, but he wasn't. "Not really, Byron, I was too young."

"What if I told you that that earthquake wasn't natural?"

"I don't know. What if?"

"The Loma Prieta earthquake was caused by A-Sync, a tech

company in San Jose working on top secret projects for the shadow organization controlling FEMA."

I'd heard this before. Not this story specifically, but San Francisco is crawling with conspiracy theorists. I can't tell you how many otherwise sane, intelligent people I've met there who honestly believe in idiocy like chem trails. "Wow, Byron," I said, trying my hardest to seem interested, supportive, calming. "So, they made an earthquake machine."

"No, no, no..." Byron began riding another wave of agitation. "The earthquake was an unexpected consequence. The earthquake happened when they opened the threshold." He proceeded to launch into a frantic diatribe about a pocket dimension called The Backrooms. "I've been there," was his ultimate reveal. "I dropped in for the first time about a month ago, but now it's happening more frequently." He described wandering for what felt like an eternity through a maze of walls covered in yellow wallpaper, flickering yellow light coming from canned recesses above, and damp, mildewing carpet below. "I'm afraid. I don't want to go back. There are... things in there." And by "things" he meant dangers in addition to the faceless men in hazmat suits.

I was intrigued, but I wasn't buying it. I asked Byron for a few hits of LSD and told him to take care of himself before slinking back inside the club. The "Missing Person" fliers with his picture on them popped up a week or two later, plastering every phone pole south of Market Street. I had no idea at the time that we'd cross paths again, briefly, in someplace far, far away. Someplace that might not even exist.

But people disappearing from the Bay Area isn't anything new. Whether they fall into pocket dimensions, pits of despair, or vanish into thin air, people do... evaporate. And most of the time, it's nothing nefarious. People go missing because they want to. Sometimes they're gone forever and other times you see them a year or two later, covered in new tattoos. Sometimes you meet the same people in different bodies, although you need to be on LSD to know for certain. And I knew I'd disappear one day too.

Still, I was struck by how Byron's description of The Backrooms was similar to Leviathan's Labyrinth as epitomized in the glorious panoramic image made iconic by *Hellbound: Hellraiser II*, at least thematically. Both are sprawling mazes of sinister liminal hallways, rooms, and corridors. Their pathways are littered with relics, oppressively ominous, and teaming with residents that exist in states beyond our understanding of chemistry and physics.

In other ways, The Backroom were antithetical to Leviathan's Labyrinth. More like a manifestation of the principals of white torture established in Iran, Venezuela, and the USA. A method of manipulation more insidious than physical torture, white torture leaves the body intact, warping only the mind. It's based on sensory deprivation and, no, I'm not referring to those ridiculous pods in those trendy salons. Victims live in a completely neutral environment: Walls, bed, food, noise, lighting. Everything is neutral. Now there's nothing where something should be. Audio, visual, and olfactory hallucinations commence. Soon every sense is scrambled, including balance and pressure. It's amazing how quickly this primitive technique breaks even the strongest constitutions, not only breeding paranoid psychosis, but rewiring a person's brains so that they never actually recover.

The main principal of white torture is: Leave no mark. Truly, a manifestation of Hell for those of us who adore both natural and accelerated forms of scarification. I don't think I'd survive. I hope Byron is okay.

Ten years had passed since I quit Sacramento City College in order to pursue loftier aspiration, but I still hadn't made any true progress in my attempts to push the boundaries of psychological and physical sensations. I had yet to find my tribe. I had casual friends. I had lovers. I had enemies. Most of them were simple props to occupy my time. I had adventures. I crashed a car in Chattanooga and made quite a scene at a horror convention in Texas. But when I'd lie awake at night, taking stock, I'd realize I had no true allies. More disheartening, I didn't have a leader, or a teacher, or a master or even a mentor. No proof of worlds beyond or within. No God. No Gods. No Leviathan levitating above the Labyrinth, shaped like a diamond, spinning, shining beams of pure darkness like a bizarro lighthouse.

I was in The Power Exchange, San Francisco's most notorious sex club, the first time I saw a God—and He was certainly the first one to take notice of me. It was Ladies Only Night. I was tied to a bed, bruised and blistered and striped with raised welts. I'd been stripped, whipped, and fisted. I was under a spotlight. I was on seven drops of liquid LSD.

My God's arrival was heralded by His Harbinger, a lithe man wearing a black latex bodysuit and a mask. A variation of your typical gimp-mask, it was made from drab, olive-green canvas. There was your standard zipper mouth, but the mesh eyes-holes were surrounded by black triangles like a clown. There was another, upside-down triangle over the nose. The mask sported bunny-ears and long dreadlocks, though it was impossible to tell whether the hair was ornamental or real. He carried a machete. He walked slowly to my bedside. Even slower, he bent down to softly breathe into my ear.

"He sees you," he told me, barely audible, in a slow monotone whisper. His words swirled into a cacophony, rising in volume before striking a crescendo. The light disappeared. A mighty curtain was dropped and I stared gasping into the hostile chasm, the hideous maw, The Abyss. I teetered at its edge as bolts of blue lightning cracked the expansive blackness.

"Behold!"

I was in the presence of The Great Pendulum, awestruck and aghast. Its mighty, intricate weight sliced through the void with a force great enough to cause shockwaves. Though intrinsically basic, it was as massive and mesmerizing. Its umbilicus alone was miles long. And as it vacillated between extremes, between light and dark, Heaven and Hell, it showed me a sign. Perched at its fixed point, atop tons of jagged earth crumbling into boulders, as though plucked from our planet with unfathomable force, clear as the eye could see, unmistakable. A great pyramid, the Eiffel Tower, New York City skyline, a space needle, and all of the other unmistakable landmarks: The Las Vegas Strip.

Already soaring above new platitudes, The Great Pendulum spoke. It was a single word. A name actually. It hit like the blast from a jet engine, bathing me in hot caustic vapors, a screaming foghorn in each ear.

"Hauptnadel."

No context but no confusion. Nothing but the clearest communication. Implicit in its singular enunciation was a message, instructions, commands: Find My God's Ambassador. Embrace him as your Earthly Master. Claim your destiny.

And so I did. And so I have. And all of creation has marveled at my suffering.

My name is Sybil.

The Brutal Black Pain Syndicate

My path from Northern California to Las Vegas was anything but a straight line and it wasn't my first significant pilgrimage.

Do you want to hear the cute and sexy story about how I got my first tattoo? Well then fuck right off, because that story doesn't exist.

Because I'm not an extreme version of your Suicide Girl fantasy lover. I'm not trying to redefine beauty. Beauty is, at best, a weapon. At worst, it's a curse, a pathogen, a disease, a death sentence. When you're beautiful, beautiful like the magazines want us to be, every man who fucks you will either love you or hate you. Nothing in between. I wanted to obliterate beauty. I wanted to make the spectrum that divides beauty from hideousness irrelevant. I never asked to be your sad seductive Goth Ophelia, unaware of how wonderful I am, waiting for you to coax me out of my shell whether I'm willing to admit it or not. Your expectations are dangerous—for both of us!

Pavia, Lombardy, Italy. It has a population of about seventy-five-thousand. Its Cathedral, established in 1488, has a dome that's ninety-seven meters tall. The University of Pavia was established in 1361 and houses an impressive museum. It had been a garrison of the Roman Empire and the Capital of the Longobard Empire. The city had once been invaded by Charlemagne but also saw Hari II crowned King of Italy. It's beautiful, though most travelers would agree there isn't a whole lot to do there. But I wasn't interested in the history, the architecture, or the cuisine.

You could stay in Pavia for weeks and never know that it had become something of a dark beacon for those seeking to redefine the parameters of physical sensations.

For years, I had dreamed about being tattooed. Not having specific tattoos really, just being tattooed. How couldn't I be drawn to an art form so inextricably bound to pain? Since I was a little girl, I've been attracted to people with tattoos. Not to the people, necessarily, but to the tattoos. I wanted to touch them. "Did it hurt?" I would inevitably ask, reveling in the inevitable response, "Of course it did!" The only ones who claimed otherwise were liars. I could smell it. As a little girl, I liked to poke myself with needles, fantasizing about my coming of age, and my first time under the gun. I'd spend hours sketching out our elaborate designs. I drew on my arms and legs with Sharpies and Bics. But I turned eighteen, then twenty, then twenty-five and I still hadn't gotten my first tattoo.

Because a part of me had grown to resent tattoos. The simple act of getting a tattoo had become a source of consternation. Tattoos were everywhere. What had once been a renegade form of self-expression became par for the course with my generation. There was nothing intrinsically shocking or confrontational about having a tattoo anymore. It wasn't almost expected. It was almost more rebellious to resist the mainstream and avoid tattoos.

I met an alternative model at a horror convention in Stockton. She had a complete sleeve done to show her love for *Hellraiser*.

And I was hypnotized by the hours of pain and talent that had gone into the assemblage. The original Cenobite quartet climbed her upper arm: Butterball (in sunglasses) below Chatterer (1987 version) below Female (Barbie Wilde version) below Pinhead crowing out the prime bicep, sporting his trademark sinister grin. The Lament configuration in his hands, almost as though he's offering it to me. Frank Cotton, wearing his brother's face is stretched by chains on her hand. Smiling gleefully. Julia, just as beautiful without any skin, watches stoically from the wrist. Merging top and bottom at the elbow, devious Dr. Channard. And, scurrying around amongst them all, The Engineer.

"What do you think?" she asked me. "Go ahead. You can touch it." Exquisite. The needlework, fine lines, brilliant shading and deep haunting blacks. It must have taken months, maybe even years to complete. And she had more tattoos, was mostly tattooed actually. Her other arm was another incongruent cluster of cinematic horror villains, her neck covered with a quote from *Fight Club*. Her legs... I never even got around to looking at her legs because even her face was tattooed. "Do you like it?"

"No..."

"No?" she repeated with a scoff. "You sure look like you like it."

"Yeah, no... Yes, I like the art. It's amazing." She smiled. Then I continued, "But I think it's a total waste of good suffering."

"Excuse me?"

"You heard me. You like *Hellraiser*?"

"Obviously I like *Hellraiser*," she replied indignantly, crossing her arms across her chest.

"Really connected with the Cenobites, I see."

"Of course! They're the best part of the movies."

"Oh yeah? Well, I think you need to go back and watch the

movie, because you clearly didn't understand the point. And please, at the very least, read *The Hellbound Heart*."

"Okay, who is this lady?" the model began looking around for her handler.

"Do you think if Pinhead was here, right now, he'd like your tattoo?"

"Of course! It's a tribute to him. I showed it to Doug Bradley at Monsterpalooza and he loved it."

"Oh, I'm sure Doug Bradley loved it, but I wasn't asking about him. The Hell Priest! Do you think he'd like it?"

"Okay..." the model threw her hands up. "Where's Reggie?"

"The Hell Priest would seethe at your weak tribute, would take offense at its blasphemous iconography, would delight in flaying your skin."

"Yeah, she's crazy. Can someone call, security?"

I shouldn't have been so hard on her. Her heart was in the right place, probably. But there's no way she had actually given thought as to what it would actually mean to become a Cenobite. If she had, if she had truly understood Barker's implications, she would have seen her folly.

My words that day, and my actions, I regret them. I was still young, finding myself, refining my voice. The acid I had been taking that day wasn't exceptional. I had no knowledge of The Great Pendulum or my destiny yet. But now, one of my core tenets is respecting other people's right to live a life of their own choosing. Just as the path I chose isn't for everybody (obviously), I will never begrudge another. If getting tattoos of your favorite movie characters brings you joy, I support it. Any form of consensual bloodletting, I support it.

And even when I was conflicted about tattoos I still loved tattoos. I still craved them and would gravitate towards anyone who had more than just a few of them, just as I had done when I was a child. That fallen soul, for example, that sad man who claims I molested him, he had quite a few tattoos, for example. I couldn't see them in a traditional sense, but I could smell the ink embedded in his body, could sense spectrum or multiple pigments.

Over the years, I'd watched tattooing grow from a fad into a high-art empire. General societal acceptance has its advantages. Of course, full-body tattoos intrigue me most. I especially love geometry, anything intricate, really. Lines contorting into the body's curves, sometimes bold and sometimes delicate. And sometimes only dots. But of all the styles over all the years, the only one that feels even remotely pure to me, is blackout.

Blackout, or blackwork, is pretty much exactly what it sounds like: Solid black covering a substantial swath or perhaps an entire limb, completely saturating the skin. It takes a lot more ink than your typical tattoo and the experience can be fierce. Increased damage to the skin results from covering the same areas repeatedly in order to achieve a desired result. Often, blackout tattoos include a subtle pattern, leaving traces of skin that are as thin as traditional tattoo lines, creating a striking juxtapositions. Sometimes, blackout tattoos are later adorned with scars or brands to create a raised, three-dimensional affect. Though shocking to behold, blackout tattoos are the perfect antidote for cutesy, hip skin-art and a remedy for tattoo-regret. While I have no research to confirm this, I suspect blackout was forged as an outcry against tattoo removal.

Maybe you're a fifty-year-old guy, and you've been getting tattooed a few times a year since you were sixteen years old. And you've accumulated an enviable amount of ink that, from a distance, looks pretty fucking cool. But up close, it's chaos, a slipshod patchwork, fractured moments of time scattered like random photographs at the mouth of a dumpster. You've got the money, and tattoo removal clinics are almost as common as tattoo parlors. Why not just erase your mistakes? I say, "Bite your tongue!" Erasing a tattoo is just as painful as receiving one, and in the end, you have nothing to show for it. Absurd! A waste of good suffering! Blackout, on the other hand, offers an alternative, a form of re-set that doesn't undo the past, doesn't deprive a person of their beautiful scars.

What about in the case of gang affiliation or human trafficking of Holocaust survivors? Would I deny them or begrudge them for seeking tattoo removal? Of course not. While extreme, the principals of blackout tattooing are not extremist. And the principals of blackout aren't universal, they aren't designed to be. This isn't a form of organized religion. It's an alternative lifestyle for those seeking more than simple adornment, more than vanity. Complete transformation. Evolution. New flesh.

I first learned about the Brutal Black Suffering Syndicate on Vice.com, just like everybody else. This extreme art project was founded by Australian tattoo artist Clancy Stewart and his Italian counterpart, Valero, in 2013. While well-versed and skilled at a myriad of styles and techniques, the team was at the forefront of the blackout movement, establishing themselves as true pioneers. They became revolutionaries and radicals. Disciples of discomfort, alchemists of agony, priests of pain. If you're lucky enough, you can find them in Pavia.

"The most important thing is the experience," Clancy explained on Vice. "To call it a rite of passage is an understatement. It's a ritual designed for those who want to push their bodies past all limits. I bring a sense of focus. Valero brings the pain."

Whereas Clancy is a jovial renegade, Valero is a monster.

"My job is to bring the pain," the Italian mammoth explains. "Your job is to take it. Sometimes, I insult people. I say, 'What the fuck are you doing? Quit squirming! Get back down on the table! I haven't finished with you yet!'" It doesn't cost a penny or a lira. Those invited to participate need only obey the instructions of these savage practitioners. "Once they go beyond their limits," he continued in his native tongue, "it becomes something new. In that moment, they have become something new. Something they never imagined."

Clancy, Valero, and their team of interns don't simply tattoo those donating their skin to the project. They ravage them. The needles are huge, industrial sized, designed to turn an epidermis into something akin to ground meat. They abandon any attempt at precision and conform in favor of deeply penetrating rakes and slashes. Blood rises in subtle geysers of red mist. They don't use stencils, discuss a plan of attack, or ask preferences from their clients.

Vice introduced us to Frankie, a tattoo enthusiast from Holland who was in Pavia for his fifth and final session with the Brutal Black Suffering Syndicate. "I feel more complete after each visit," he explained. Frankie is already largely transformed. His neck, shoulders, chest, arms and face all show the signs of Clancy and Valero's special brand of beautification. Yet even this repeat visitor, this man whose eyeballs are also tattooed black, couldn't endure the ritual in its entirety. A planned four-hour session had to be abandoned after three. Franke is pulled from the table, sick and trembling. His body and face look like they have been taking shrapnel. His blood drips black. His wounds are wrapped in plastic before he's tossed back into a cold world. The ritual has left the studio smeared in ink, sweat, and bodily fluids.

"That's it!" Valero screams after Frankie's departure. "No more! Never again! Fuck these cowards!"

The Vice article that introduced us to the Brutal Black Suffering Syndicate also announced the project's retirement. I was devastated. Like a child who had just seen a commercial for the greatest amusement park on Earth before being told they could never, ever visit it.

"We've decided to throw in the towel," Clancy explains, "before our project becomes diluted."

The sense of loss was excruciating. It wasn't fair. I wanted

Clancy and Valero, needed them, knew I could be the warm body of their dreams, their adoring acolyte. I wouldn't disappoint them. And I'd finally be able to sport tattoos I could be proud of, body art that accurately reflected my intensions and ideologies. I wept and bemoaned and lashed out before deciding, no. I would find Clancy and Valero. I would find them and convince them to perform one last ritual. I wouldn't take no for an answer.

I got off my train in Pavia, jumped in the first Taxi I came to, and spoke the only word of Italian I had bothered to learn: "*Tatuaggio*." The driver knew exactly where I wanted to go.

Clancy could have been a pirate in a past life. Hell, he could be a pirate in this life. His head is completely bald except for a pristinely curled handlebar mustache. He's got a gold front tooth. His scalp, forehead, cheeks and chin are a quilt of tribal designs, coded mantras, and secret symbolism. And in spite of his flare, his "peacockery", his most striking feature is his smile. Completely charming.

"Sorry, love. The suffering Syndicate's been abandoned." He stood on the other side of the front counter. Their studio, a perfectly dark and dreary temple, somehow much larger than its tight parameters. Wooden paneling throughout, red and black candles, the walls displaying the shop's history through a greatest hits montage captured in high art photographs. In back, a tattoo gun hissed. A woman with blonde dreadlocks squired as Valero, his back to me, blessed her with his needle. "I can put you on the waitlist, love, but we don't have any openings until November. Or I could recommend a bloke I know, a blackout artist in Milan. Maybe he could take you on."

"No," I replied with more force than I intended, surprising even myself. "No," I repeated somewhat more composed. "It has to be you." In back, Valero's tattoo needle went silent, so I know he was listening.

"Don't know what to tell you, love," Clancy said. "Even if

we could see you now, it wouldn't be the experience you saw on the Internet. The project's over." In back, Valero's tattoo needle went back to work. The woman who was already significantly inked, was having her nipples outlined in an intricate design.

"I know why you stopped," I continued. "I know that you were disappointed in the results. Because people didn't understand what made your project so important."

"So what is it then, love? What made our project 'so important'?"

"Ritual."

There was a pause. Both Clancy and Valero's tattoo gun fell silent as if considering. Then the tattoo gun went back to work, a blonde woman went back to straining. Then Clancy made a face that told me, "It's not just up to me, love." He jerked his head backwards in Valero's direction.

Even before I met them, before this telling interaction. the Vice report made it clear: Clancy was the voice of the Brutal Black Suffering Syndicate, but Valero was the star talent. More than that, he was the soul of the operation and its High Priest. He didn't just specialize in blackout, he lived it, with just about every inch of skin below his nose thoroughly soaked in black ink, including his ears. A demigod, an ambassador of higher forces, a natural sorcerer, a true and truly dangerous artist.

"Please, Valero," I called back to him. "Please!"

The mountain of a man turned his head over his shoulder. Not enough so that he could see me, but enough so that I could see him. He turned up his nose and inhaled loudly and slowly through his nostrils before saying something in Italian. Clancy and the blonde lady laughed.

"What did he say?" I asked.

"Well, love, he says you smell like a lawsuit." More laughter as Valero's gun went back to work.

"Please, Valero!" I persisted. "I can pay you." And then, in what was, at the time, my most seductive intonation, I said, "I'll do anything." But these words succeeded only in poking the bear beyond annoyance. Valero stood up so violently his chair flew backwards. He turned and moved towards me so abruptly, his long beard picked up air. He took his place besides Clancy, dwarfing his partner, and slammed his fists on the table like a gorilla.

"No! He screamed. "What don't you understand? We don't want you rich bitch Instagram fuck sluts in Pavia! Go home before you get wounded!"

I opened my mouth to reply, but Clancy's eyes begged me not to. Still, I stood my ground for a moment, locking into Valero's furious gaze, his smoldering hatred. One second felt like an hour. Two seconds felt like a year. Three seconds and I spilled out of the shop, practically falling out the front door, and out back onto the streets of Pavia.

I checked into a hostel to drop some acid and contemplate my next move. I was put into a room with a couple of British bisexuals and a lesbian from Hungary.

What, you didn't think I could be so easily deterred, did you? Do I strike you as someone who only takes things half way? I'd sold just about all of my worldly possessions in order to get to Italy. Now that I had arrived, I figured I could stay for up to a month if I was careful with money.

Words. They can be so fucking manipulative. Valero told me, "Go home before you get wounded!" Not, "Go home before you get hurt!" So what's the difference? Tremendous. I could ask anyone to hurt me any way at any time. But being wounded is a world beyond. I enjoyed pain, obviously, but I didn't want Clancy and Valero to hurt me. I wanted them to wound me, irrevocably wreck me, give me an experience likely to knock my psyche into cosmic wormholes. "Go home before you get wounded!" It was a test.

When a gentile seeks to convert to Judaism, they seek counsel with a Rabbi. They will ask, "Can I be a Jew?" and the

Rabbi will reply, "No." If the gentile returns a second time to ask, "Can I be a Jew?" the Rabbi will once again reply, "No." But if the gentile seeks counsel with the Rabbi a third time in order to ask, "Can I be a Jew?" the Rabbi will ask, "Why do you want to be a Jew?" If the gentile can articulate a response that incorporates the primary teachings of the Torah, they will be invited to convert. Rituals completed, they will be a Jew.

So like a gentile asking a Rabbi if I can be a Jew, I stood in the doorway of Clancy and Valero's studio every morning for over a week. And when Clancy would sigh and Valero would scream, I'd move only as far away as the shop's only window, where I'd watch them with religious vivacity despite an extremely limited view. Clancy always seemed sympathetic, but Valero grew increasingly irate, sometimes spitting on me as he passed, once even throwing a hot cappuccino at my chest. And as his furious bellowing grew, so did my commitment. Deprived of my desire, my longing grew until my need was genuine, multiplied, intensified, sanctified.

It took me eleven days to provoke an elevated response from Valero. Not quite the response I was expecting, but it did the trick. First, he threw me into the shop and pushed me up against the wall, all the while, Clancy was trying to restrain him. Then he attempted to squeeze his finger into my septum ring. It may have been easier for a camel to travel through the eye of a needle than for Valero to stick his giant digit through my ring (sizable though it may be). Still, it was enough for him to get a grip and he jerked me upward, by my nose, with almost enough force to pull my feet from the floor.

"Why do you come here every day? Why do you pester us? Why do you come here every day?" He was seething. Spittle rained down on his beard and his eyes become so bloodshot they seemed to glow red. I met his gaze, unflinching, my septum proving resilient enough to withstand his manhandling.

"Put her down, mate," Clancy counseled his partner.

Valero ignored him, keeping his anger focused on my face. "Do you want me to hurt you?" the ogre inquired.

"No," I responded. "I want you to wound me." The troll released his hold. "I need the ritual," I told him calmly. His eyes turned cloudy, cool, alien. "I'd walk through Hell for this," I insisted. "Please," I implored. "Please be my Priest."

Valero rubbed his chin and, while keeping his eyes on me, asked Clancy a question in Italian.

"I dunno, mate. Seems a bit cruel."

"I don't care," I inserted. "Whatever it is, I'll do it. I'll do anything."

Valero looked at Clancy, and then back at me, weighing opposing viewpoints in order to pass his final judgment. And after a few moments of silence, he spoke. "I have rules."

"Anything." I assured him.

"No drugs. No food. No drink. No smoking. No sex. And no sleep for two days and 12 hours."

"I swear," I said with guttural sincerity, devastating appreciation.

"If you lie to me, I will know," the hobgoblin cautioned.

"I swear," I reiterated.

Clancy softly sighed, shook his head, and stared solemnly at the floor.

The Brutal Black Pain Syndicate doesn't operate in the same open area of the shop where Clancy, Valero, and their protégés normally work. A ritual this intimate, this extreme, requires its own room. No windows and the walls are paneled in smooth black walnut. Throughout the room are photos of sessions past. In one, Valero holds a woman's vagina open, stretching her vulva into a butterfly. All of her pink and more has been replace by the deepest black. The blackout explodes from her loins onto her belly, hips, and thighs. Exquisite.

The room had been prepared with candles, incense, and all the appropriate tools and supplies required. Two tattoo guns sat on trays, surrounded by cups of pitch-black ink, ready to ignite. My altar, little more than an unforgiving wooden plank covered in layers of saran wrap. I laid myself down, naked except for a pair of white cotton panties. And I was elated. Because this was to be a dream come true. I feared weeping with utter joy before the process had even commenced. Finally! My first tattoo!

Soon, I was surrounded. Valero and Clancy at me feet, two ominous assistants at my head. In footage on Vice, I'd seen the duo work with one helper, once in a while, but never two. I suspected this meant they had something special in mind for me. I imagined each man attacking me, two at my ankles and two at my wrists, savaging my skin until they all met up together at my navel. They did have something special in store for me. But it was not the treatment I imagined.

"Lorenzo and Mattia are here to hold you down," Valero explained of his henchmen.

"You won't need to hold me down," I promised.

Valero laughed, heartily, almost vivacious. Soon, Lorenzo and Mattia were cackling along. Clancy just sighed and shook his head. "You said you would walk through Hell for this," my Priest pontificated.

"I would walk through Hell for this," I assured him.

"After tonight," Valero explained, "You'll walk through Hell forever."

Lorenzo and Mattia held me down, each incapacitating a shoulder, pinning me to my plank. Clancy and Valero turned on their machines and proceeded to tattoo the bottoms of my feet. The clocks froze and the Earth stopped spinning. As nanoseconds dragged, the first row of the first gun began to pierce the sole of my left foot. Penetrating the uppermost layer of epidermis, the needles scratched a previously insatiable itch. My eyes rolled into the back of my head, my spine arched, and I came. But everything changed before the first second of the ritual had passed.

There are over three-hundred-thousand pain receptors on the bottom of each foot, packed more densely than on any other part of the body. That's why stepping on a Lego feels insane. That's what made my experience so extraordinary. When both men were tattooing me in unison, arced like a stream of electricity. Had Lorenzo and Mattia not been there to hold me down, I might have involuntarily broken my own spine. It was a level of pain I didn't know existed, a level of pain intensified by my willingness to take it. A level of pain beyond pain. I was terrified.

Stephen King's short story, "The Jaunt" was published in his *Skeleton Crew* collection, released in 1985. It imagines a world where interplanetary travel has been made possible with teleportation technology. Taking a trip is called "Jaunting" and travelers must be unconscious. This is because the process is instantaneous for the body, but nearly infinite for the mind. Anyone who jaunts without adequate anesthesia will go insane. A young, curious traveler decides that he wants to experience the unknown and holds his breath when an attendant attempted to administer gas. When the young passenger arrives on Mars, his body is withered, his hair is white, and his mind is shattered. Unable to articulate millions of years of disembodied solitude, he can do little more than cackle and claw his eyes out.

The Suffering Syndicate took four hours completing my ritual but it felt like a thousand years. If I hadn't been held down, I most certainly would have clawed my own eyes out.

They tattooed the bottom of my feet. They only tattooed the bottom of my feet. For four hours straight.

There's a chart online that illustrates the most painful places to receive tattoos. The armpits, the kneecaps, and the nipples rank among the most extreme. But the soles of the feet can't even be quantified. And don't remind me that Miley Cyrus has a tattoo on the sole of her foot, because it's not remotely the same. Her practitioner was quick and made her as comfortable as possible. And it's small. My practitioners were fiends dedicated to my discomfort, determined to destroy me. Their needles plunged so deep and with such veracity, they hit bones in my feet. They broke bone, chipping away little pieces that still float in my flesh like shards of broken glass. Of course I screamed for them to stop. Eventually, they put a gag in my mouth.

"No stop! No safe word! This is what you asked for!" Valero bellowed, slamming his fist against the wall.

As Clancy appeared to be completing my right foot, Valero screamed and struck his partner square in the jaw. "It's not black enough!" Valero screamed. "It must be black! Black! Do it again from the beginning!" As the needles minced the soles of my feet, repeatedly, even tearing at the webbing between my toes, I lost control of my bodily functions. My period started two and a half weeks early. I periodically went deaf and blind. I would pass out only for the pain to immediately snap me back into consciousness without a nano-moment's reprieve. Mucus ran from my nose like a waterfall. I strained and howled like a soul possessed by Pazuzu. All of my muscles melted, my bones were ground down to sand. My very molecules became incohesive and I disintegrated into a quantum foam of unimaginable intensity. And just before I died from dehydration and exhaustion, it was over.

If there was a way of quantifying pain, I would have set a new world record. Beyond that. I didn't know it then, couldn't have known, that my pain was so profound, so significant, it resonated on a cosmic level. I had become a light, visible to otherworldly forces.

It was nearing 6 AM in Pavia when Valero tenderly dressed my quivering, blubbering form and took me in his arms. Like a sick child or an injured animal, he cradled me, my head resting limply against his warm, mammoth chest. I could hear birds chirping as we walked through the streets, away from his shop. When he was certain no one had seen us, he dropped me on the sidewalk, spit on my back, and abandoned me. Obviously, I couldn't walk, so I crawled four kilometers back to my hostel on my elbows and knees. When the manager found me on the lobby floor, he called an ambulance.

At the hospital, they asked me if I had been attacked. Though obviously recovering from trauma, they couldn't figure out what was wrong with me. Not until the black blood started seeping through my shoes. My cotton socks had fused to my feet, cemented by dried tissue fluid, coagulation, and puss. When the peeled them off of me, I was thrust back into searing pits of white-hot agony.

I had expected Clancy and Valero to begin at my jawline (or my hairline) and work their way down. I expected to emerge from my transformation slashed in black saturation across my arms, breasts and legs. I expected to be a walking testament to the pain I had endured. Instead, I had endured the unimaginable, been obliterated and reassembled—and I had nothing to show for it. Nothing, except looking like I've just walked through an oil slick in bare feet.

Beware of what you wish for and never meet your idols? Bite your tongue! I'm indescribably grateful for my time spent with The Brutal Black Suffering Syndicate. It wasn't what I expected, but it was exactly what I needed. Clancy and Valero taught me a valuable lesson about vanity and pride. They changed me forever. They transformed me. It was exactly what I had asked for.

More importantly, I now realize that this experience set everything else into motion, facilitating my eventual communion with The Great Pendulum.

I was so broke that I had to return to America on a cargo ship out of Lisbon. On quiet nights crossing the Atlantic, I'd drop mega-doses of LSD I had scored in Ibiza before sitting on deck and singing to the humpback whales.

I sang to them in their native languages.

Five Questions

"What would you say if I told you I could change your entire life forever by asking you five questions?" Larry asked me.

I had just finished loading the last of my belongings into my truck. My plan was to catch a nap on the couch before hitting the road for Las Vegas first thing in the morning before sunrise, as commanded by The Great Pendulum.

"Shit, Larry. Please don't tell me you've become a Jehovah's Witness," I replied.

Larry was one of my roommates. We shared a not-quite-legal converted warehouse with four others. All of us considered ourselves artists of some sort: A photographer, a filmmaker, a dominatrix, and a guy who created sound collages out of lost media. Larry was a programmer, a gamer, plugged into his computer for hours on end, melting into one of those expensive office chairs with the high backs and built-in speakers. He was in his mid-thirties and had a 19-year-old girlfriend who stayed over often and orgasmed loudly. He also played the sitar, both for pleasure and income, performing weekly at an Indian restaurant in Citrus Heights. I don't normally feel the need to identify people racially but, in this case, I think it's important to note that Larry isn't Indian. He's white.

"Ha, ha, ha, no," Larry responded, not laughing, but actual saying "ha, ha, ha" with snarky sincerity.

Larry was just a pound or two above scrawny. He had long hair that he wore exclusively in a tight ponytail. He was a bit of a comedian. Literally. He frequented open mics where he could work out his newest material.

"I don't know Larry. I guess I'd say I'm about to leave my entire life behind to go hunt for Bigfoot in the redwoods. I'm pretty sure my life is about to change forever anyway, so what's the point?" I got comfortable on the living room couch where I planned to sleep for about four or five hours. Larry took a seat in one of the tattered recliners on the other side of the coffee table, almost directly across from me. None of the other roommates appeared to be home. But they were.

"Come on," he plied with a smile. "Humor me. What if I told you I could change your life forever by asking you five 'yes' or 'no' questions? That if you answer 'yes' to all five of the questions I ask you, you will see the world, the entire universe in a new light? That it would change everything?" He was smiling, but there was an intense undercurrent subtlety building.

"Is this a game, Larry?" I asked, opening a bottle of beer and lighting a cigarette.

Larry thought for a moment before replying, "Okay, you can think about it like a game. It's more of a thought experiment, but we can make a game out of it, sure."

"Does it matter that I dropped acid a few hours ago?"

"Not at all," he assured me. "It might help actually."

"Well, in that case..." I pulled a vial of liquid LSD out of my pocket and put another drop on my tongue. Just a refresher. Not enough to prevent me from driving in the morning, even if it prevented me from sleeping.

Larry laughed, an actual laugh. Almost a giggle. I had taken the bait. Now he had to reel me in. "So since this is a game, let's make it interesting."

"If you suggest stripping again I'll fucking stab you."

"Stop it, come on," he persisted.

"What did you have in mind?" I asked.

"Let's gamble."

"You know I'm broke as shit, right?"

"Not money," Larry replied in an attempt to sound enticing and mysterious that actually sounded creepy.

"What then?" I asked, suddenly feeling the need to cross my arms across my chest.

"If you answer 'yes' to all five of these questions, and you agree that I have changed your life forever, and you see the world in a whole new light..." he paused for dramatic effect and raised a single eyebrow. "Then you sign a billion-year contract pledging your eternal loyalty."

"Oh fuck, Larry," I gasped as I sprung to my feet, fearing it was worse than Jesus. "You're a fucking Scientologist."

"No, no, no," Larry assured me, imploring me to sit. "It's a game, remember? I mean, it's a billion-year contract. There's no way that's enforceable, right? Not unless we live forever."

"Is that one of the questions?"

"Ha, ha, no."

If I hadn't just taken that last hit, I might have just shut it all down. Told Larry that I wasn't interested in a theological or cosmic debate. Reminded myself that sleep was more important than playing games with my sleazy roommate. Damn, though, he was reeling me in.

"I don't know, Larry," I said in a last half-hearted act of resistance. "Can you ask me the first question so I can know for sure this isn't about Scientology?"

He thought for a moment, almost as if he was waiting for someone to give him the correct response in an earpiece, and said, "Sure. Okay. The first question is:"

another dramatic pause, "Is it possible to simulate consciousness?"

I was so relieved I laughed out loud. I don't think he'd ever heard me laugh before. I'm not sure any of my roommates had. Larry seemed a bit shocked and disappointed. "So you're talking about The Matrix?"

"No, no, no," he replied. "Actually, we call it Simulation Theory." When not gaming, fucking his girlfriend, or playing the sitar, Larry spent hours on a sub-reddit called NoneOfThisIsReal. They'd get into heated online arguments that got so intense you'd think that the fate of the universe was at stake. I hadn't noticed that he'd been spending more and more time in that forum, obsessing. I'd been so focused on my impending move to Vegas, I didn't notice that his girlfriend hadn't been coming around much, if at all. And where were my other roommates? None of them had active social lives, spending most of their off-time right here, in the living room. Was I missing something?

I certainly had no idea about the "Five Questions Internet Challenge" that had been linked to a recent suicide cluster in Reno.

I was wired. My gears were spinning. "Well, if all we're talking about is simulations and theories, fine." I told him. He had reeled me in. I was in the boat. Now he wanted to club me.

Did I believe it was possible to simulate human consciousness? "Well, LSD was simulated. I guess anything is possible."

"So is that 'yes'?" Larry replied with glee and a hint of neediness, "I need you to say 'yes'."

"Yes, Larry," I said with an eye roll. "You're one-fifth of the way to having me as your slave." As if I could ever serve anyone or anything besides The Great Pendulum.

"I never asked for your servitude," he shot back, just a bit too wounded. "Just your loyalty. And it's not even me, per se."

As if my loyalty could possibly be questioned or subverted by a silly game. "Okay, Larry, I apologize. I'll try to take this seriously."

"Because you should," he shot back, quickly baring his teeth before smiling, regaining his composure. "I mean, it's more fun this way."

"Okay, Larry, I said, quickly retreating to the kitchen for another beer and then returning." I was having fun, toying with this nerd, entertaining his feeble attempts to intrigue me. Except I was intrigued. Intrigued immensely by the concept of consciousness and expanding it, often tripping into rabbit holes with those who can keep my attention. "I'm ready for Question Number Two."

"Will technology continue to advance into the conceivable future?"

"Don't see why not," I responded before quickly correcting myself. "Yes, Larry. Technology will continue to expand into the conceivable future. Why wouldn't it, except for an apocalypse or something."

Larry was pleased. He began to smile like an amateur magician with a secret. I was still intrigued, but not remotely expecting an actual life-changing epiphany. Not after what I had so recently seen at The Power Exchange.

"Are you ready for Question Number Three?" he asked me.

I said, "I am," because I was. Happy to play word games, mind games with some crazy character I'd never see again after tonight. I was flying with a beer buzz and colorful visuals. It was a fine way to pass some time.

"Can advanced civilizations continue to evolve indefinitely without destroying themselves?"

"God damn I fucking hope so," I blurted out, again requiring correction. "Yes." Yes I've always been a nihilist, but I'm also a utopian. I truly believe a unified society would have epic potential. If I didn't at least believe it was potentially possible, what would be the point? Of going to Vegas? Of anything? Might as well sacrifice myself to The Great Pendulum on the spot.

Larry's smile grew ever wider, inflamed by LSD that made it appear as if he had suddenly grown a second row of teeth. It was a little frightening, Larry's smile and the fact that I had now said yes three times. It was time to proceed with caution.

"Will advanced civilizations want to run simulations?" he posited, now struggling to retain his giddiness.

"Now, by 'advanced civilizations' are you talking about humans, or...?"

"Yes, humans," Larry replied before correcting himself slightly. "Humans and post-humans."

Was that an important distinction? "What's a post-human? You mean like that baby at the end of 2001: A Space Odyssey?" The cretin probably didn't know Kubrick.

"Sure, why not."

"Okay, glad I asked. Because the second you mention aliens, I'm going to bed. Scientology or not."

"So what's your answer?" Larry plied, eager to snag the fourth yes.

If this was going to go down to the wire, it was time to put on my game face. "Yes. Advanced human civilizations will want to run simulations. Why wouldn't they?"

Larry was practically besides himself with joy, unable to contain himself. To him, the game was all but won. Poor fuck. He was going to be pissed when he came to collect my loyalty, only to find I have nothing left to give him, committed so thoroughly and inextricably to The Great Pendulum. But just in case...

"You don't actually have a contract, do you?"

"Actually, I have one right here," he replied, producing a document from his lap as though it had been there the whole time. He handed it to me across the coffee table.

It was huge. Heavy and dense with stipulations. But LSD had robbed me of my ability to read. Every page of this document, my supposed contract, was a stream of random letters and numbers. And they were moving. Changing. Like a malevolent virus attempting to decipher cryptography, searching for the right combination to break a lock. "How the fuck am I supposed to read this?" I asked a prematurely gloating Larry.

"What's it matter?" he replied. "It's just a game, and it only matters if we live forever. And don't forget what I promised you: You'll never see the world, the universe in the same light again. Your life is about to change."

Yes, my life was about to change. Thanks to The Great Pendulum. I thought, "Soon this game will be over, we'll all have a chuckle, and I'll have time to grab a few hours of rest before leaving Sacramento forever, probably."

As Larry prepared to ask me his fifth and final question and I prepared to put my loyalty to a higher power on the line, the atmosphere went still. My enhanced LSD-vision allowed me to see individual specs of dust suspended throughout the room, as though frozen. We lived near a freeway and had become accustom to the static sound of constant traffic. Suddenly there was none. Nothing else made a sound either. No dogs, no birds, no neighbors shouting in the distance, no machinery rattling. It had already been dark for hours, but it somehow became even darker. Oppressively dark, creating storm clouds in my peripheral vision.

"Are you ready?" he asked me, sitting upright, his fingers digging into the arms of the recliner.

I crossed my arms over my chest and said, "Yes, I'm ready."

"You can't lie to me," he warned. "I'll know if you're lying."

"I won't lie," I assured him. Because I wouldn't have to lie. Because it didn't really matter. Because this is a game. What was I actually afraid of? Getting sucked into The Matrix or worse, becoming a Scientologist?

"Don't look so scared," he said with a mocking undertone. "The last question is the easiest." A moment of dead silence before the words issued forth with the cool emotionlessness of a robot. "Would an advanced civilization capable of running simulations want to run a lot of them?"

It felt like a loss in cabin pressure. Because not only was my answer yes, but the full ramifications of all five questions in their entirety became crystal clear. Larry was over the moon. Because I had just proven, by my own words and my own reasoning, that we are all in a simulation. It's not something that may hypothetically happen in the future, it's happening now. This is it and this is everything.

"My God," I gasped.

"Say it!" Larry commanded. "You can't lie to me!

"Yes."

"Because?"

"Because if an advanced civilization is running multiple, simultaneous simulation, in all probability..." Larry and I completed the sentence together.

"...we are in a simulation."

The contract was in my lap. A pen was in my hand. And I was collapsing into myself.

"It's okay," said a woman's voice, soothing me. It was Mary, another one of my roommates, the dominatrix. She was followed by Sarah, Manny, and Shannon, my other roommates. We were all here now, and everyone took a seat in the living room. Manny and Shannon sat on the couch, one on each side of me. "We were all scared at first too. But it's okay," Mary assured me.

"Sign the contract," Larry commanded.

"Come on, sweetie," Mary cooed. "Sign the contract."

My eyes ran from Mary and Larry to Sarah, Manny, and Shannon. "Sign," each one chanted as eye contact was established. "Sign."

"And what happens then?" I asked through shaking breath and shuddering muscles. I was cold.

"That's the wonderful part," Mary beamed. "You get to reset. Start over. Live your entire life over again. Now that doesn't sound so bad, does it?"

"No," I grudgingly admitted. But what about this life, I wondered? What about my great plans? "What happens if I don't sign it?" I asked. "Hypothetically."

Shannon, Sarah, Larry, and Manny hissed, a sudden shocking chorus. Mary soured.

"You listen to me," she began in a cold, monotone. "This reality, this version that you have always existed in? It's an experiment."

"For what?" I asked, mostly just to hear the sound of my own voice.

"This is an experiment in torture. But not epic, hellish torture like you're so fond of in your movies. This is soft torture, subtle torture, a lifetime of random degradations and constant indignities, solely designed to inflict suffering without a trace. And the end result is, inevitably, that you will go completely, painfully insane."

"How do you know all of this?"

"Because I'm part of the simulation, you primitive twat!" Mary screamed, suddenly unhinged and impatient. "Sign the fucking contract! You made a bargain, you said yes five times. The scales have been lifted from your eyes." Mary's voice was contorting into something inhuman. "Sign the fucking contract!"

And it was at my lowest, just as I touched pen to paper, trembling, confused, defeated, that I received a series of mighty revelations like a shockwave.

Wormwood, MK Ultra, The Montauk Project, to name just a few. LSD may have never achieved cultural significance if it hadn't been for the CIA. They eventually began studies in

Universities like Stanford where LSD was first consumed by the likes of Dennis Leary and Ken Kesey. The CIA believed LSD was a shortcut to mind control, for creating super soldiers and Manchurian Candidates. How ironic then that those who participated in these experiments often emerged no longer scared of death or submissive to authority? A bus full of Merry Pranksters spread the word from coast to coast, bringing psychedelia to America and, eventually, the world.

People say it all the time: "I've learned so much from taking LSD." They're talking about universal truths that suddenly shine like supernovas, evaporating the constant smog of deception and manufactured consent. It's as though LSD confirms what we already suspected, but also reveals hidden knowledge—information that changes your perception forever.

Poets sometimes describe themselves as vessels, claiming they are but conduits for truths revealed by a higher power. A poet on LSD makes for a powerful warrior.

I don't know for sure if it was LSD granting me access to volumes of complex philosophies, if I was a vessel for a higher force, or if this was all due to the direct intervention of The Great Pendulum. But I now knew for certain: This was a test.

And I had almost failed.

"No!" I shouted. A cacophony of hissing commenced.

"It's too late for no!" Larry screamed.

"It's too late for no!" Mary repeated, her voice now truly demonic.

"Not just no," I countered, "but five times no! No, no, no, no, no!" Unbridled conviction. Still, my roommates all laughed at me.

"Look at her," Mary scolded, "Attempting to put the genie back in the bottle. Trying to close Pandora's Box after she's learned the truth."

"There is no genie," I replied. "No genie, no bottle, no box." My roommates laughed again in nearly robotic unison, louder.

The wind picked up outside indicating a storm was coming. "It's pure arrogance to think that we would know what a post-human society would do," I continued. "I don't believe for a moment that they'd waste what would have to be nearly god-like powers on simulating potential universes. And to what end? Impossible!"

My roommates continued laughing, but something was off now. They were out of sync. Less enthusiastic. Even more robotic.

"We have seen them with our own eyes!" Larry stated.

"We have met our Masters!" Mary insisted.

"Maybe so," I replied. "But you haven't met mine." The wind outside intensified. Then came the sound of rain and static, soft until it became furious.

"But you know it's true!" Larry and Mary roared in unison. "You said yes and yes and yes and yes and yes!"

True, I had said yes all those times, taken a ladder into insanity one rung at a time. The descent softened by years of *Star Trek* and heady science fiction that actually convinced me that the universe was something more than vast, frozen, dead space. But now I saw the light, and I was free."

"Well now I say no, motherfuckers!" A bolt of lightning followed by a clap of thunder. "Because it is impossible for humans or even post-humans to simulate consciousness. It will never be possible."

"Absurd!" was Larry's retort.

"Let me ask you a question, Larry: How can humans simulate consciousness when we can't even agree on what consciousness actual is?"

"Ye of little faith!" he scoffed. "You don't believe in the godlike potential of your own species, the infinite possibilities this universe creates."

"No, Larry. I don't believe humans are godlike and humans can never be gods. And while I suspect mankind will continue making technological progress for a few more centuries or decades, I don't think we can evolve indefinitely without destroying ourselves. I mean, just look around. There are too many great filters we'll never be able to overcome: Nuclear war, environmental disaster, our inevitable inability to reach 94% of the perceivable universe. And in a few million years, there won't even be a single trace that we ever existed." The laughing robots were growing agitated, uncertain. Uncertain perhaps of what was happening and who they were. "Life is paradoxically self-destructive."

"Fool!" Larry screamed. "We're evolving at speeds never before imagined or conceived. We will proceed by great bounds never before taken in the history of our planet. Simulating consciousness is already within our grasp. In the future, it will destroy all physical limitations!"

"No." I responded with a gleeful vindictiveness. "It won't. I'm sorry to break it to you Larry, but you won't live forever. None of you will." They didn't want to accept anything that contradicted what they had been promised. Promised, not by Larry, but by whomever was pulling his strings. Whispering into his ear. Cold, hard, facts: There will never be a digital afterlife, a new-age paradise for them to rejoice in forever. No magical upload. Not now. Not ever.

I believe in transhumanism. I welcome the next stage of human evolution. I seek physical and psychological transformations. But I can never accept this brand of metaphysical techno futurism. Metaphysics as a scam, a con that imagines infinity isn't an obstacle, that immortality can be stipulated. Will we colonize our solar system? Probably. Will we open and artificial black hole and obliterate the universe? Maybe. Will new gods or old gods bring Hell to earth? Without a doubt. But we will never exist within The Matrix.

Manny and Shannon got up off the couch, rubbing their eyes and twisting fingers in their ears. Sarah was crying. The demon inside Mary's mouth was retching. Outside I almost believed a tornado was about to set upon us. I had to raise my voice to be heard over the ruckus. At this point, I wasn't talking to anyone in particular. I was on autopilot. I was a vessel.

"For the sake of argument, let's say you can generate consciousness by simulating a brain. If you count every interaction between synapses as one operation, your brain runs at the power about ten to the power of seventeen. That's one hundred million billion operations per second. It takes ten to the power of twenty operations just to simulate one second of human consciousness. If we want to simulate more than just one human, but the entirety of human history, three-hundred billion humans with an average life-span of fifty years then consider this: One year has thirty million seconds times fifty years times two-hundred-billion humans times ten to the power of twenty operations. We'd need a computer able to handle a million-trillion-trillion-trillion operations per second. That's more operations than there are stars in the observable universe. A computer like this is just impossible."

"Ha!" Larry scoffed, as though I had actually proven his point. "A Matrioshka Brain computer encapsulates a star. A megastructure of this size feeding of cosmic radiation could easily perform a million-trillion-trillion-trillion operations per second. More than that in fact—easily!"

Poor, poor Larry. His feeble mind muddled. "That's pure science-fiction. It's physically impossible."

"Not for a post-human society," Larry insisted. "In fact, we wouldn't even need something that big. An advanced human civilization could construct a Matrioshka Brain computer that's only the size of a city."

"Are you listening to yourself? Even a computer the size of a city, a small city, is pure fantasy. Give it up, Larry. You're lost."

"Where am I?" muttered Manny.

"What's happening?" asked Shannon, as if waking from a trance.

"I'm going to bed," said Sarah.

These three stood up slowly and walked out of the room, backwards, the same way they had entered. Mary remained indignant, stomping her feet.

"Liar!" Mary screamed. "Cheater! Blasphemer! Heretic!"

A pained look came over Larry's face, like he had consumed an ice-cold beverage too quickly. His eyes fluttered. His neck twitched. If he were indeed a robot, this was the moment he would have started saying, 'Error, does not compute' as smoke shot out of his ears. I expected his head to start spinning any moment. But he had one trick left up his sleeve.

"If we're not in a simulation, then how can I do this?" Larry stood up, closed his eyes, and stretched out his arms. He began hyperventilating. Then he held his breath until his face turned red. He began to flatten and elongate. His entire physical form began to disappear and reappear in a rapid flutter. His skin color changed from blue to green, from yellow to orange, from violet to red. It was a stunning display.

"God damn, this is some good acid!" I exalted, undaunted by Larry's cuttlefish display.

There was a flash of light outside. The power within cut out for a few seconds. When the lights came back on, Mary was gone.

Larry produced a cell phone from his pocket. He dialed a number and held it up to his ear.

"Who the fuck are you calling?" I asked him, only to be ignored. Larry turned his back to me, but I could hear him speaking:

"Have you been watching this? I don't understand... But you said... I don't know what to do..." Larry's eyes got wide. He pulled the phone away from his ear, turned back around and informed me, "He wants to speak to you." He held the phone out to me, but I didn't budge. A second later, Larry put his caller on speaker phone.

"Hello lovely," said the voice from Larry's device. "Creating quite a ruckus I see." The voice was male. Calm, controlled, and condescending. I didn't respond. "You have quite a mind, I must admit. You've thrown us a bit of a loop. But you said yes five times. That means we own you." And then, for a moment, his voice became fierce and evil. "Now sign the fucking contract!"

"I won't sign the fucking contract," I replied.

The voice on the phone laughed. It laughed and laughed the most hideous laughter I'd ever heard. "In that case, we'll be seeing you soon."

"You'll see me in Hell," I replied.

The phone went dead. Larry, defeated, looked at me with a mix of anger and trepidation.

"Larry, remember when I threatened to stab you earlier this evening?" Before I had even finished asking my question, I had produced a switchblade from the pocket of my hoodie, pressed the button, and stuck the blade into Larry's abdomen on his left side. He gasped. His eyes were wide as saucers. The blade went in with ease, producing a crisp wet sound when imbedded. It felt nice. So I stabbed him again. And again. The fourth time I pushed the blade inside him, I left it inserted and rotated the handle a few times. Then for flare, I gave him a slit here and a gash there. His shirt began to drip. Larry stumbled backwards, falling into a heap on the floor.

"You tried to put my universe into your nutshell, and I will not stand for it."

Outside, the wind had subsided. Normal noises had resumed. The traffic, the dogs, the noisy neighbors—everything was as it had been before. The dawn was approaching. And so I took my leave.

I wasn't trying to kill Larry necessarily. I only intended to punish him. And to give him something to remember him by. But I cut too deeply.

As for the man whose voice I heard on Larry's phone, I'm not afraid of him either. He should be afraid of me. Because I'm not the "lovely" girl he and his followers tormented on that night. I've transformed into something more powerful than he could have ever imagined.

Find me if you dare.

Death Valley

Most people traveling from Sacramento to Las Vegas would use a GPS device or Google Maps or some alternative app to plot their course. My route was dictated by The Great Pendulum. He marked my way with special breadcrumbs only I could identify, unmistakable markers that left no room for misinterpretation.

Since Larry died, I was advised to skip the most obvious thoroughfares. I was guided deep into the Eldorado National Forest before backtracking through the Stanislaus National Forest, then abruptly east again through Yosemite National Park. LSD made this leg of the journey immaculate. Falls bursting from cliffs, illuminated from behind by a sunset that turned the water blood red. But this was no sightseeing expedition.

I zigged through the Sierra National Forest, zagged through Kings Canyon National Park, then shot abruptly north over Mt. Pinchot and Mt. Thompson. I kept to the speed limit and avoided cameras at gas stations. I drove mostly at night, pulling off onto logging roads to sleep during the day. When I had reception, I'd look for updates regarding my situation online. The news named me a person of interest in Larry's demise. At this point, they weren't sure if I was a perpetrator or another victim, on the run or the subject of a kidnapping. None of my roommates had been able to give a coherent account of that evening's events. When they discussed me, the used my birth name. But she isn't me anymore. My name is Sybil now, as ordained by The Great Pendulum.

My God's Harbinger waved me down at a rest stop outside Manzanar. His face remained the same: The canvas mask with rough black stitching, the zipper mouth, the dreadlocks, the bunt ears. But his body was now clad in an Armani suit stylishly paired with an expensive trench coat. Moonlight glistened on the buckles of his shoes. He instructed me to take 395 South in order to pick up a hitchhiker near the foothills of Waucoba Mountain.

I found him at around 3:30 the next morning, a man on the side of the highway wearing a plague doctors mask made entirely out of feathers. I pulled over, rolled down my window, and honked my horn.

"Burning Man is over!" I ribbed as he approached my vehicle.

"He told me you were coming," said the hitchhiker as he ambled towards my vehicle. "The man with the bunny ears. The Harbinger." He continued, as if there had not been any question about whom he was speaking. "He wants me to take you on a trip. He wants me to show you something."

The hitchhiker removed his mask. Without this odd adornment, he looked pretty quintessential. A desert dweller, a drifter, weathered and wise. His hair was a tangled mop, his beard long and bleached by the sun. He might have been in his twenties or in his fifties, an old soul or an old man, It was impossible to tell. His clothes were caked in layers of mud and dust. There was a backpack slung over his shoulder, a worn briefcase in his right hand, and an old mechanical typewriter at the end of a short chain locked around the hitchhiker's left ankle. The clunky apparatus dragged behind him when he walked, resulting in a stuttered, limping gait. He threw most of his gear into the backseat before lifting his anchor by the chain and making himself as comfortable as possible in the passage seat beside me.

"First thing's first," I stated before getting back on the road. "What's your name?"

He thought for a moment and replied, "You can call me DJ."

"Hi DJ. I'm Sybil. Nice to meet you." We shook hands. "Next question: What's up with that typewriter on your leg? That can't be comfortable."

"I'm a writer," he explained without any further elaboration.

"Of course you are. Obviously."

DJ, the writer, had a thousand-yard stare. Now that he was sitting beside me, I noticed blood under his fingernails and bruises under his eyes. I was reminded that hundreds of horror movies began like this: The solo driver picking up the random stranger out in the middle of nowhere. But I wasn't afraid. Sure, I had my trusty switchblade in my pocket, but I also knew that we had been brought together by a grand design, connected by the direct intervention of The Great Pendulum.

"Where are we going?" I asked once his seatbelt was securely fastened.

"Death Valley."

Nestled between the Mojave Desert and the Great Basin, the area was appropriately dubbed Death Valley by a group of silver miners in 1849. Thirteen of their peers perished in a wagon train attempting to transverse the unforgiving desert. Death Valley still lives up to its moniker. The desert continues to kill. Often. It covers over three-thousand square miles and, today, Death Valley is home to fewer than three hundred permanent residents, making it one of the most desolate places on the planet. At its lowest point, Death Valley sits at two-hundred and eighty-two feet below sea level, a record for the

Northern Hemisphere. Temperatures break world records, topping out at one-hundred and thirty-four-degrees Fahrenheit. Before the California Gold Rush inspired prospectors to willingly subject themselves to these hellish conditions, the region was populated by the Timbisha tribe of Native Americans, formerly known as the Panamint Shoshone, for over a millennium.

Ghost towns remain including Panamint City, Ballarat, Chloride City, Leadfield, Randsburg, Greenwater, Harrisburg, and Skidoo. Some of the intrepid explorers who visit these abandoned outposts report seeing their shadows separating from their bodies, acting on their own accord. Steer clear of the Amargosa Opera House and Hotel, established in 1923, near Death Valley Junction if you're sensitive to or easily disturbed by spectral imprints. Rooms 24, 32, and 9 are said to be extraordinarily active. In bed, at night, guests report the sensation of their feet being held down when trying to fall asleep. Campers throughout the region describe feeling as though something has slithered into their sleeping bags, seeing orbs on the roadways and lights in the sky in the dead of night.

Before the greedy miners and even before the Panamint Shoshone, The Great Basin was inhabited by a loosely connected collective of nomadic tribes call the Paiute. They called this region home for three-thousand years. For centuries, storytellers spoke of a great underground city, an ancient race, the Empire of the mighty King Shin-au-av. They called this "God's Land" and "Ghost Land". Legends tell of a great chieftain, so distraught over the death of his wife he doubted life was still worth living. He made the decision to deliver his earthly body to the Land of the Dead. When he finally found passage below the mountains, he was greeted by a glorious maiden. She was the daughter of Shin-au-av, the mighty subterranean King. She was able to heal his heart with a combination of sacred roots and secret rituals. The chieftain returned to his people reborn, regaling his people with tales of the wonder and beauty found in the Kingdom of Shin-au-av.

The sun rose in the east as DJ the writer and I left all of civilization behind us. "Want some LSD?" I offered, producing a vial of clear liquid from my pocket.

"I have something even better," he told me, retrieving his cracked and tattered briefcase. He spun the numbers of its built-in combination lock, pressed a couple of buttons, and the case popped open. A golden glow seemed to emanate from within. I saw the entirety of Hamilton's Pharmacopeia and so much more. I marveled. I salivated. I became sexually aroused. "But we'll have to wait until the hour is correct," DJ said with just a hint of condemnation. "Patience, please."

I understood. "You're a shaman, aren't you?"

DJ considered for a moment before responding. "Yes. I am. By definition if not by design. I have such sights to show you."

In the upper pocket of the opened briefcase, I spied a stack of manilla folders and loose papers, both typed and hand written. "What's all that?" I asked.

"Research. For my next book."

"What's it about?"

"Drugs," he replied. "Drugs and subterranean civilizations. And a girl who gets lost in the desert."

"I'm intrigued," I admitted. "Tell me a story."

"Oh, you want to hear a story?" DJ the writer asked with boyish excitement in his voice and demeanor. "Here's a story for you..."

Since I picked him up near the foothills of Waucoba Mountain, my passenger had been mostly quiet, radiating a distant yet focused intensity. Now he was Mr. Chatterbox. Writers certainly do enjoy telling their stories.

"Mummies! Giants! Underground Civilizations!" DJ had the enthusiasm and dramatic cadence of a full-time podcaster. "Shall I continue?"

"You must continue," I assured him.

"Well, this story I'm about to tell you is pretty much the strangest thing I've ever heard."

"Stop teasing me!"

"A couple of conservationists were exploring the Wingate Pass area of Death Valley. Let's call them Bob and Jack. On their third day of hiking, Jack fell through a mine shaft, something that had been abandoned back in the 1890s. When Bob climbed a rope down in order to rescue his companion, they discovered a cavern leading into a sprawling cave system. Well, they followed those caves northward, towards the Panamint Mountains. They lost time in there. Days maybe. Jack would later say they simply felt compelled to push onwards. Well, after covering a distance of over twenty miles, they found themselves in the grandest chamber they could have possibly imagined. And what do you think they found?" the writer asked me with glee, bursting to reveal.

"I couldn't possibly..."

"They found a huge, ancient, underground city!" DJ exclaimed before I could even finish my sentence.

"Wow."

"Yeah, wow!" the scribe rejoiced, his eyes widening, his voice cracking. "Now get this: Everything was illuminated by an ingenious system of lights fed by subterranean gasses. Even after thousands of years, streets were lit and homes were warm. They went through manors and castles and cathedrals before finding a burial chamber. Inside were seven extremely well-preserved mummies. The climate in Death Valley is perfect for natural mummification, so this discovery alone wasn't earth shattering. What wasn't normal, what challenged our very understanding of ourselves as a species, was their sizes. Between eight and eleven feet tall. Can you imagine it?"

"I am," I promised. "I'm imagining it right now. Tell me more."

"Except for the mummies, the entire city appeared to be empty and vacant, a fact that was both a disappointment and a relief. How wondrous it would have been to establish contact with a lost civilization. Wondrous and terrifying. Still, their discoveries were as numerous as they were valuable and culturally relevant. They explored manors and castles and cathedrals, chambers whose purpose couldn't even be construed. Massive stone doors were that were perfectly counterbalanced revealed temples, altars, and arks. Council rooms contained polished stone tables for meeting and stages for open debates. And so much treasure: gold statues, vaults and stone drawers filled with gold bars and galaxies of rare gems. They grabbed a handful before finding corridors leading upward and out, eventually emerging from a tunnel-like quay about half way up the eastern slope of the Panamint Mountains. Way off in the distance, they could barley make out Furnace Creek at the bottom of the valley."

"What did they do then?" I prodded.

"They contacted the Smithsonian and the Institution sent a representative to interview the explorers. Jack and Bob told him everything and gave the administrator the gems they had recovered as proof. But that was a big mistake. The Smithsonian has a reputation for suppressing any information that surfaces about giants—especially those discovered in America. They never saw those gems again and the Smithsonian later denied every interacting with the duo."

"Why does the Smithsonian want to suppress information about ancient giants?"

"That's another story all together."

"Okay, fine. So what did Bob and Jack do next?"

"Well, before they vanished off the face of the planet, they mounted another expedition to the Panamint Mountain range. They brought a team of local scientists and potential investors. But when they returned, they couldn't find the quay they had emerged from. There had been a freak cloudburst that summer, a thunderstorm that dropped so much rain, the entire landscape had shifted. Though obviously humiliated, Jack and Bob were last seen looking for additional quays at higher elevations. But they were never seen again. It was like the mountain swallowed them whole. And while the men are hardly the first to go missing while exploring Death Valley's brutal landscape, I like to imagine that they found their way back to their subterranean utopia. I like to imagine that they're still there."

"Damn."

"But wait! There's more!" DJ was nearly frantic and I was genuinely rapt. The writer re-opened his briefcase and produced a newspaper clipping. "I found this in an issue of The San Diego Union published in August 1947, just a few years after Bob and Jack went missing."

"What does it say?"

DJ the writer had to squint and focus in order to read the fading, smudged text of his yellowed article. "The headline reads: 'Trace of Giants Found in Desert'. Okay: 'A retired doctor from Ohio has discovered relics of an ancient civilization whose men were between 8 and 9 feet tall, in the Colorado desert near the Arizona-Nevada-California line, an associate said today. Howard Hill of Los Angeles, speaking before the Transportation Club, disclosed that several well-preserved mummies were taken yesterday from caverns in an area roughly 180 miles square, extending throughout much of southern Nevada all the way into California's Death Valley. Hill said the discoverer is Dr. F. Bruce Russell, a retired Cincinnati physician, who stumbled on the nest of several tunnels in 1931, soon after coming west and deciding to try mining for his health.' Okay, then there's a sub heading that reads: 'Mummies Found.' It's a little hard to make out here, but it says that Dr. Russell only fully explored these caverns in 1946. He brought a famous archeologist with him, a guy named Dr. Daniel Bovee who discovered cliff dwellings in New Mexico. Dr. Bovee confirmed Dr. Russell's discoveries, stating that, in his opinion, the mummies and other artifacts were at least eighty-thousand-years-old."

"Amazing!"

"Right? Then there's this quote from Dr. Hill about the mummies: 'These giants are clothed in garments consisting of a medium length jacket and trousers extending slightly below the knees. The texture of these materials is similar to gray dyed sheepskin but obviously it was taken from an animal that is unknown today.' Then there's another sub-headline that says, 'Markings discovered'."

"What's it say?"

"'Hill said that in another cavern was found the ritual hall of the ancient people together with devices and markings similar to those now used by the Masonic Order.'"

I balked at the mention of Freemasons. "That can't be true," I said, straining to read the weathered article myself while driving, craning my neck over to DJ's side of the vehicle.

"That's what it says," DJ insisted, pointing out the text in question. "Shall I continue?"

"Of course."

"'In another long tunnel were well-preserved remains of animals including elephants and tigers. So far, Hill added, no women have been found.'"

"Bummer."

"Okay, this last part is really interesting: 'Hill said that the explorers believe that what they have found is the burial chamber of the civilizations' hierarchy. Hieroglyphics, he added, bare a resemblance to what is known of those from the lost continent of Atlantis...'"

"Okay, now you can just shut the fuck up. I let you off the hook for that stuff about the Masons, but I draw the line at Atlantis."

"Don't you want to know how everything turned out? What happened to the mummies and the follow-up expeditions?"

"What happened to the mummies and the follow-up expeditions?" I asked with a sigh and a roll of my eyes.

"Gone. Disappeared. The mummies and Dr. Russell. His car was found in a remote corner of Death Valley miles away from where his caverns were discovered. And, of course, no one else has been able to find the tunnel systems he described."

"Of course."

"We're here."

We pulled into the parking lot for one of the few legitimate tourist destinations in Death Valley. But there are no rangers here. No daily tours. No air-conditioned museum offering knowledge and respite. Just a couple of unisex bathrooms. I parked close to the wooden platform that crosses the sink, the small saltwater pond whose undrinkable waters gave this location its name. Badwater Basin.

There was nothing to see these days. While the waters that normally accumulate here contain plantlike and animal life, mostly snails, years of drought left it empty, muddy, paste-like, poisonous sludge. We looked at the wooden elevation sign:

BADWATER BASIN
282 FEET / 85.5 METERS
BELOW SEA LEVEL

"And look over there," DJ the writer pointed to a sheer cliff, miles behind the parking lot. There was a huge line painted on the face of it along with towering letters that still looked small:

SEA LEVEL

From there, we sauntered down the walkway that leads about 100 yards into the basin, and this is where the desert becomes truly wondrous. Quintessential apocalyptic pornography, the wasteland every dystopian saga desires to duplicate. Consistent rain and evaporation cycles pull salt crystals to the surface, drying in hexagonal honeycomb patterns. The sun was high and the expanse was harrowing, so brightly illuminated it seemed like a white void at its parameters.

"This is what you wanted to show me?" I asked.

"This is the first step. We need to get to the lowest point." DJ pulled a pair of sunglasses out of his flannel shirt. His trusty briefcase at his side, the clunky typewriter around his ankle, my guide smiled.

"I thought this is the lowest point?" I said pointing back at the sign and the line.

"That sign's a liar," the writer informed me. "The real low point is about ten miles west of here." He pointed. "You might want to go back to your truck and put some shoes on."

I had already wrapped myself like a mummy in rolls of black cotton fabric to protect myself from the Sun's destructive rays. I had capped my head in a woven hat that had a ridiculously oversized brim. My nose was slathered in SPF 72. But my feet were bare, as I preferred it.

"I'll be fine," I assured him.

"The sand can heat up to over two-hundred degrees. It'll feel like walking through Hell."

"It always does," I assured him. "After you."

For hours the writer pushed forward, dragging that ridiculous artifact attached to his leg, that stupid typewriter. I appreciated the obvious metaphor and DJ's commitment to suffering, but I also appreciate dispensing frivolity in the name of practicality. Still, I followed dutifully behind him in a state of muted excruciation. It had been years since my session with the Brutal Black Suffering Syndicate, but my feet would never heal completely. Scabs begat blood blisters begat abscesses. Pus would flow like little rivers beside streams of black ooze. They had tattooed my feet hard enough to chip my bones. Every few weeks, a shard would attempt to eject itself through the ball of my foot or the heal. It feels like being cut with glass from the inside out. Every step was a reminder of what had happened, what I had endured, and the lessons I had learned. This journey into the depth of Badwater Basin was no different. The pain was immense. And, as always, I was grateful.

"We're here," DJ the shaman-scribe announced. He held out his arm, smiled, and did a little twirl.

"How can you tell?"

"I can feel it. Can't you feel it?"

I closed my eyes, turned my face to the sun, and inhaled the salty, acrid air. "Yeah, I suppose I can."

"Come on. Let's get ready."

It was my job to get a fire started before sunset. DJ's job was to prepare our potions. He opened his briefcase, giving me another look at the splendor within. I saw vials of pristine liquids along with jars of plants, roots, and spores. There were the usual suspects: LSD, psilocybin, PCP, ketamine, cannabis, and disco biscuits. There were more exotic delectables as well: Bufotenine, synthetic Ibogaine, Kratom, mescaline, peyote, Salvia Divinorium, toad venom, DMT and, of course, Ayahuasca. I even saw a canister of Xenon.

"You're obviously familiar with LSD," DJ ventured as I made a small teepee of twigs over a couple handfuls of dried scrub.

"Obviously."

"And is it safe for me to assume that you're familiar with many more of these?" he asked, motioning to his opened briefcase.

"It is."

DJ began pulling specific jars and arranging them in smaller subsets. "My job tonight is to give you the most intense psycho-spiritual experience of your life. To that end, I must assemble a concoction specifically tailored to your unique lifeforce. I must take into account your emotions, culture, experience, spirit, and sensations."

"How do you do that?"

"I do it by reading your aura."

I wished him luck with that.

The sun was disappearing behind the mountains in the west. DJ and I sat across the fire from one another. He looked deep into my eyes for minutes at a time before turning to his pharmacopeia for an ingredient. A pinch of this, a dash of that. A spore, a leaf, and a pellet. A dash of liquid. All of these and more were mashed into a sticky paste in my shaman's stainless-steel mortar and pestle bowl set, a necessary accessory for any apothecary. He mixed the paste with water, creating a scintillating tincture which he proceeded to divide into two small cups.

"Bottoms up," DJ signaled before downing his cup. I had expected more of a ritual. Still, I never hesitated. To call the potion bitter hardly conveys its putrescence. And even though it wasn't a heated blend, it felt hot—almost sharp. My body tried to rebel. My throat tightened as my esophagus attempted to gag it out of me. I wouldn't allow it! I pushed, choked, heaved, gasped, but I was able to guide the brew into my stomach. Not that it would stay there for very long.

I vomited tar and blood and bile. Vines emerged from the desert floor to suck up the chunky liquid before returning silently into the sand. I vomited snakes and frogs and salamanders. I vomited a race of slimy homunculi who scattered, screaming into every corner of the basin. I vomited hooks and chains that shot past the basin floor, through a tiny portal, and into another realm. The pain intensified until I writhed and contorted, tearing at my clothes, my face, and my hair. And all the while, DJ sat in silence, meditating like a monk, tuning into the eternal motion of The Great Pendulum.

Everything went black. I could hear my heart beat slowing, feel my lungs clenching, sense my brain unraveling. Educated psychonauts refer to this moment as Ego Death, and it's a necessity for any truly meaningful exploration. It's the moment when you accept your inevitable demise, allowing you to see the universe without subjective emotional attachments. I had experienced it before, hundreds of times. But this time it was different. Some LSD users talk about a point of no return, a moment when you either submit to insanity or claw your way out like your life depends on it—because it does. I had experienced that feeling as well, a dozen times at least. But this time it was different. It felt like I was pushing an unknown boundary past its limit. I was scared.

"Did you know..." There was a voice in the darkness. It was DJ the writer. Except it wasn't. The voice was slower, lower, saturated in flange and echoes. "...that millions of years ago..." The voice was throaty, distorted, almost artificial. "...this entire basin..." It was the voice of a demon or a demigod "...was an ocean."

I opened my eyes as cosmic symphonies consumed me. The sky was alight with stars, planets, comets, and meteors. Entire galaxies unfurled their arms to embrace me. There was a sudden gush, an immense pressure that almost popped my body before I acclimated. DJ and I were at the bottom of the ocean. An abundance of life emerged before our eyes, creatures outlined in translucent lasers of rainbow light and geometric lens flares. They were of every era: Dinosaurs, giant jellyfish with quivering tendrils, a tribe of lamprey, coelacanths and frilled sharks. A horde of manhole-sized horseshoe crabs scurried across the basin, maneuvering around me, my shaman, and our campfire. And there were more, so many more. Manta rays as big as stealth bombers, school of stunning sturgeons, shellfish of unimaginable shapes and sizes, squid and octopi spinning. Swimming, gliding, diving. An entire undersea world superimposed over reality, its grandeur on full display.

"What can you tell me.." DJ's eyes had turned completely black. "...about whales?"

"Whales are mammals," we said in unison. Pods of every whale species and subspecies swam by us, filling the night with their myriad songs.

"This is an indohyus." DJ spoke and the sky turned black, erasing our aquatic world. A small, pig-like animal hopped, scurried, and groomed itself in the slate-colored expanse above us. "He's the size of a cat," the demonic voice continued. "But this order of raoellidae would go on to evolve into the most enormous animals to ever live on Planet Earth." I wasn't expected to speak, only to listen. "What do you suppose..." DJ posited, "...persuaded this species to throw away half a billion years of evolution in order to return to the ocean? Were they scared off the land by something unimaginable? Were they called out to sea by something unexplainable? Did they know something?" As he spoke, the indohyus morphed, changed, grew exponentially and evolved, epoch by epoch, until a lone blue whale danced in the sky. All the stars and more retuned to shower the noble animal in resplendence. "Are they smarter than us?"

DJ was wearing his plague doctor mask constructed entirely out of feathers again. I didn't see him put it on. Just one instant he wasn't wearing it and in the next instance he was. Then, in another instant, he was wearing a burlap sack over his entire head, cinched around his neck with a noose. Then he was wearing the mask of my God's Harbinger: drab olive canvas crafted to hug his skull with specificity, mesh eyes adorned with diamonds, dreadlocks floating, bunny ears twitching. He unzipped his mouth and a colony of bats blasted out, swarming me before scattering into the atmosphere.

"The desert is full of holes." DJ still had the voice of a

demon. Now, though, I could also sense empathy. Connection. Soft but unmistakable urgency. "There are mines and caves and tunnels below us. They run down through The Mojave, through Joshua Tree, to The Salton Sea—the Land of Lithium. There are tunnels that run to Las Vegas. And beyond."

In another moment, DJ was wearing a gas mask, futuristic. There was a white flash and a mushroom cloud erupted behind the writer. The sky was crimson red. The clouds turned into smoke. The blast-wave hit me, vaporizing my clothes, melting my skin and muscles, my bones turned into dust, and wind blew me across the basin.

I returned in another moment, reassembled, redressed, sitting across the campfire from DJ. Except it wasn't DJ. He was a man with metal syringes implanted in a row across his forehead. It was a beautiful, painful halo. My Earthly Master.

"Did you know, that there are places you've never been, where you already belong?" He had an accent I couldn't recognize. Maybe Belgian, Austrian, or Hungarian. Perhaps a mix of regional dialects. "You are not alone." The words sent my hand reflexively over my quivering lips. "There are so many of us, just like you." The man with the metal syringes in his forehead smiled. "And we can't wait to meet you. We can't wait to accept you."

There was a fraction of a second of complete silence when these blissful words were spoken. Then it felt like a bomb went off. A blue lightning bolt cracked the purple-black sky, leaving the stench of scorched ozone, fragmenting the desert floor around me. I was pushed into a void that opened up behind me, falling backwards. When I hit the bottom of the shaft, I could see DJ staring down at me from a faint window within the suffocating darkness. He wasn't wearing a mask. His voice was human again, as it had been. He called down to me.

"I can't hear you!" I replied, additional bolts of lightning cracking the desert sky. DJ Called again, but now a mighty wind was howling. "I still can't hear you!" I yelled. Though I could barely make out his details from my distance, I could tell he was frustrated. This was an important message and it was imperative that I received it.

We hunt blue skies? Exalter lies? Begone white light?"

Four syllables. DJ pulled as much air into his lungs as would fit and screamed straight down the shaft at me. He took a new breath for each word, each enunciation as urgent and intense as the next. Until it was unmistakable:

"He! Wants! Your! Eyes!"

The walls of the shaft crumbled down on me. I dove into a connecting tunnel. Boulders, sand, and debris sealed me in. My time with DJ the writer, the shaman, the demon, had ended. I sat alone in complete darkness for what felt like hours.

And then, as I had hoped, he appeared to me: The Great Pendulum. Slicing through the atmosphere, creating infinite space within my claustrophobic confines.

For twenty miles, he guided me through the firmament, until we reached the gates of The Kingdom of Shin-au-av. There was a lock, a riddle, a puzzle that needed to be solved before entrance could be granted. My hands massaged the pieces, the geometric components of primitive machinery, molding stone and mineral components into soft clay, triggering a mechanism. Wheels turned and gears whirled, pulleys were activated and the mighty stone doors swung open.

And there it was in all its indescribable magnificence. The great underground city. A maze akin to Leviathan's labyrinth, yet somehow, dare I say it, even more divine. Stairways and walkways led to multiple levels as roadways and viaducts loomed, arching like birds of doom as they shifted and cracked. Homes and mansions and cathedrals. Altars and stages and celebration halls. The residents of the city were dead, but their imprints still walked the streets, speaking, singing, and debating with gusto. Conversations mixed with ambient tones creating a soothing lullaby. Yes, I wanted desperately to join them. But this was not my tribe. And so, The Great Pendulum directed me down an especially dark and isolated avenue.

Leaving the glory behind me, I walked into a tunnel that was almost perfectly circular. Before me, a powerful red light flickered. Electrical plasma jumped up and out like arms, like tentacles beckoning me inward. I could have been walking into metaphysical portal or the gaping maw of a subterranean monster. It didn't matter. So great was my trust in The Great Pendulum. So passionate was my commitment to this mission, my mission, my transformation. As I stumbled ever closer, a choir filled my ears, harmonizing in alien tones that seemed to fracture my senses. Gravity took over. And as I came into contact with the cosmic machinery of this secret entity, four words resonated in my mind.

"He wants your eyes."

Elevators to Hell

Clive Barker's other cinematic masterpiece is *Nightbreed*, released in 1990. Long before shows like *Buffy the Vampire Slayer* portrayed monsters as sympathetic antiheroes, *Nightbreed* introduced us to The Tribes of the Moon, an outcast community inhabiting a subterranean world called Midian. While it ended on a cliffhanger that suggested a franchise would follow, *Nightbreed*, based on Barker's own novel *Cabal*, was singular. There's a *Director's Cut* that most notably features a club scene with Anne Bobby singing, and a *Cabal Cut* that includes scenes culled from VHS work-tapes creating a more expansive, if uneven, movie-going experience.

Whereas the Cenobites of *Hellraiser* appeared forlorn, lonely, and cold, the monsters of Midian were a lively, vibrant, lusty society. There were many different "species" intermingling in ways that seemed artistic, ritualistic, and carnal. There was rampant hedonism mixed with all the love and drama of a huge extended family. Craig Sheffer, who would go one to play Joseph in *Hellraiser: Inferno* (where he was subjected to the erotic manipulations of The Wire Twins) plays Aaron Boone in

Nightbreed. Drawn to Midian by a series of violent nightmares, Boone is revealed to be Cabal, a prophesied leader. When the monstrous humans led by the insidious Dr. Decker, played to perfection by David Cronenberg, invade and destroy Midian it's up to Cabal to establish a new utopia. Will there be another Midian? Does one already exist? I'd like to think so.

I love *Nightbreed* almost as much as *Hellraiser*. I understand why it's become a sort of Magnum Opus for outcast communities, offering hope to the neglected and downtrodden. But I never dared to dream that there was such a community for the likes of me. I've always been the misfit among misfits. They say, "Your vibe attracts your tribe." For most of my life, my vibe has been, "Stay the fuck away from me". Fittingly, I never established a reliable, social core group. Just a string of roommates and temporary props to occupy my time. But my experience with DJ in Death Valley got me thinking, hoping, dreaming. The man with the metal syringes in his forehead, a glorious halo of pain and chemical enlightenment. Would he bring me home? Was there a Midian for the likes of Sybil? Would I finally be able to sing, scream, and rejoice with people who are genuinely like me?

I have no idea how I arrived in Las Vegas, by the way. It's possible that I teleported through an organic tesseract or cosmic portal. It's possible that DJ drove me here while I was catatonic, taking my truck as his toll. Which is fine. I didn't need it anymore. I came out of a fog to discover that I had pre-paid for a month's stay at The Whole Year Inn, a dodgy fleabag in one of Vegas's seediest sectors. The other tenants were mostly drug addicts, sex workers, and alcoholics. Sometimes they were all three. A few people, you could tell, had come to die, walking corpses who retreated into their rooms with grocery bags full of booze. I didn't get close to anyone during my stay. This was not my tribe.

My residency in Vegas wasn't idle or frivolous. The Great

Pendulum had brought me here, offering the prospect of genuine fulfillment. But nothing was guaranteed. I'd have to prove my mettle. This was my initiation phase, a period of rituals and tests designed to determine my worthiness. I came to understand that gaining audience with my God's Ambassador would be complicated and conditional. The secret sanctuary I sought could only be found by navigating an underground region of territorial sects with apocalyptic politics. And when I say that these places and people are underground, I don't merely mean outside of the mainstream, of or belonging to the fringes, mysterious and therefore taboo. When I say these places and these people are underground, I mean subterranean. Las Vegas is a portal and there are unknown worlds waiting to be explored. But they are not for the timid.

Many of these territories were pioneered by extreme mavericks with generational wealth or affiliations with clandestine government shadow groups. The 1% of the 1%. The ones who believe they've already experienced everything the known world has to offer. The ones who want to create their own worlds, craving a semblance of godliness. Spiritualists, scientists, artists, engineers, and hedonists. They've created permanent and semi-nomadic encampments, communities both sealed and open, places to visit and places to disappear into forever. For many, it's a playground. For others, it's Hell. Most groups have a charismatic leader and a transgressive, often conflicting credos. Ideologies clash. Revolutions simmer.

Societies are connected through a series of corridors and elevators, a network or "web" patrolled and presided over by a "neutral" peace-keeping contingency known as The Forlorn Order. Many of the larger casinos have direct access to this labyrinthine, often referred to as "Elevators to Hell". They all take you to the hub, a secret Las Vegas underground, a dangerous and exotic outpost called Terminal Island.

Forty-million tourists visit Las Vegas annually and most have no idea this underworld exists. Most wouldn't believe it if you told them, won't believe it even now, simply because they can't imagine it.

When I came out of my fog at The Whole Year Inn, I found the closet and drawers stocked with new clothes. There was a purse on the nightstand. It contained a wallet full of cash and a brand new cell phone. I turned it on and it rang almost immediately. I answered on the first ring.

"We see you," a voice told me. He sounded distorted but not foreboding, procedural, but not unfriendly. "Your application for passage has been received." I opened my mouth to ask whom I was speaking, but was shushed before I could utter a syllable. "Don't speak. Just listen. I am a liaison, a link in a chain. I'll be your Underseer. I'm here to guide you through your rites of passage as ordained by The Forlorn Order. If you agree, just nod."

I nodded, even if I didn't yet understand it all. The Forlorn Order, my application for passage, why rites of passage were necessary. Because mine was not to question why. Mine was but to do or die. So I'd listen to this Underseer and take his word as gospel. Whatever is necessary in order to arrive at the subterranean shores of my glorious tribe.

"Eyecandy, Mandalay Bay, 11 PM. Order a drink, then sit at the video poker table."

I nodded. Breathless.

The call ended.

I was a dive-bar Goth back in California. Eyecandy is a chic, high-tech nightclub that I wouldn't have been caught dead in. I was dressed appropriately, coiffed and stylish and, therefore, extremely uncomfortable. The clientele was predominantly programmers, entrepreneurs, and investment bankers, blasted on cocaine and seething with entitlement. Their dates were models and influencers and expensive escorts. The music was soulless way-too-loud techno drivel. It was Hell, and I don't mean that in a good way. As instructed, I purchased a drink at the bar before making my way to the video poker tables in a thankfully dark corner. I inserted an ear-piece in order to receive further instructions from my Underseer.

"Do you see the blonde woman at the bar?" he asked in his distorted whisper inaudible to all except me. Of course I did. She was stunning, glowing, her body perfectly wrapped in a black cocktail dress. The most unique feature was the eyepatch she wore. It bore a jewel-entrusted insignia. "She's going to sit beside you."

As soon as he spoke the words, the blonde woman tapped out her cigarette, gathered her belongings into an expensive, oversized purse, and made her way through the crowd. We made intense eye contact as she drew closer, sustained the locked gaze as she sat beside me.

"What now?" I asked the woman and my Underseer.

The woman reached into her purse and produced an antique metal syringe. The needle dripped shimmering liquid.

"What is it?" I asked.

"Consciousness expansion," my Underseer replied.

"Don't worry," the woman said soothingly. "This won't hurt a bit."

It wasn't that I was afraid of pain, or even needles, obviously. But I wasn't a slammer. I didn't shoot-up. That wasn't my jam. But what was I going to do? Hesitate at the precipice of the very first step of my journey? Disappoint my Underseer, and The Great Pendulum, and DJ out in the desert? Never. I rolled my arm open, revealing the soft spot in the fold between upper and lower arm, that spot where my veins rise high like pipes. The needle tore a hole and choirs began to sing.

"She has something for you," my Underseer explained. "It's a box."

The woman pulled a black lacquered box out of her bag and placed it on the table in front of us. It wasn't much bigger than a fist. There was a hole in the top and, even though the box was close and hardly shallow, I couldn't see what was inside of it. Just complete darkness. And still, a hint of motion, a subtle vibration.

"Put your hand in the box," my Underseer and the blonde woman said in unison.

"What's in the box?" I asked, my head now seriously swimming from the potion I'd been injected with.

"Murder Hornets," they replied in unison.

I didn't hesitate! I swear it! I only paused to savor the moment, anticipating new thresholds before sliding my left hand gracefully into the perfect hole carved into the top of the heavy cube. And as I did, it felt as though the hole tightened around my wrist, making extraction impossible. As if I would retreat. There was a crack of blue lightning and, for a moment, the world disappeared. I found myself floating through the void in the presence of The Great Pendulum. Another bolt exploded through the blackness and I was back at Eyecandy. The blonde woman was gone and the line to my Underseer had disconnected.

The box felt impossibly bigger on the inside, with more than ample room for me to stretch my fingers. But that only made more room for Murder Hornets, and it felt like there were hundreds of them inside.

Ritual, etiquette, repetition. These were the corner stones of my rites of passage.

Ritual: My Underseer contacts me with a location and a time. I dress according to specification and follow all preliminary instructions. I'm usually directed to bars in or near established and well-funded casinos, but I was also sent to smaller, sleazier venues downtown. I'd sit and wait for the identity of my Underseer's assistant to be revealed. It was usually a beautiful woman, but not always. It wasn't always a woman. They weren't always beautiful. They didn't always smile. Some seem scarred or recently injured. Some had undergone extensive plastic surgery. Some had faces that didn't even register. Others looked like the last person you'd ever suspect.

They always give me a shot, always from an antique metal syringe, but it wasn't always the same concoctions. Variations of singular recipe, yes, but new ingredients would be added and subtracted, like the formula was being calibrated for my personal consumption. The serums' affects had certain unalterable variables. A rush, an intensification of sensory perception, and an ego death followed by hours of inner space explorations, spelunking dark and primal psychological chasms of mercy and misery. Still, each trip was singular, unique in some regard. There could be a physical element, like pressure bearing down on me, like I was underwater. There could be a pervasive dread or a pesky paranoia attempting to push me off my course. Visuals could be light like tracers and halos or extreme, transforming humans into animals or monsters. Audio hallucinations likewise pivoted between the angelic and the abominable. Sometimes, the venom of a particular insect would interact with a seemingly random molecule with extraordinary results.

They always brought me a box, though the box was sometimes a bag or even a burlap sack. Whatever the receptacle, it seems to envelope my hand as I slide it inside. There was always a surprise inside, and rarely the same one twice. Tarantula hawk wasps, warrior wasps, red harvester ants, paper wasps, Amazon Giant Centipedes (which can eat mice), yellow jackets, puss caterpillars, bloodworms, fireworms, fire ants, cicada killers, velvet ants, executioner wasps, or combinations of them all. Once, the box was filled with water and the water teemed with lionfish.

Once, the box was a glass of water. It wasn't until I looked very closely that I saw it, translucent, floating, about the size of my pinky nail. Irukandji jellyfish are rare and can be found swimming in the waters of Northern Australia, though climate change has caused their numbers to surge. Most jellyfish can only sting from the tips of their tentacles, but Irukandji can also sting from the bell. Australian survivalist Robert Drewe says their venom is one-hundred times more potent than a cobra and one-thousand times more potent than a tarantula. The sting from an Irukandji can cause fatal brain hemorrhages. According to study by Teresa Carrette and Jamie Seymour published by James Cook University in 2011, a small amount of venom causes excruciating muscle cramps in the arms and legs, severe pain in the back and kidneys, a burning sensation of the skin and face, headaches, nausea, restlessness, sweating, vomiting, an increase in heart rate and blood pressure, and "psychological phenomena such as the feeling of impending doom." Symptoms can persist for up to seventy-two hours.

"What do I do with this?" I asked my Underseer and his assistant for the evening. My hand wouldn't fit into the glass.

"Drink it," they replied in unison.

Etiquette: Never betray your suffering by expressing discomfort. No embarrassing wincing or subtle groaning. No fidgeting. No unnatural tensing of any muscles. No trembling. No silent tears. Don't make a scene. You're in public. You're being watched. You're being judged. Keep your poise. Blend seamlessly into your surroundings. Play the games. Drink the drinks. Make polite conversation with anyone who approaches. You may be asked to sit for an hour. You may be asked to sit for a day. You may not leave your seat at any time for any reason. You may not eat. You may not relieve yourself. You may not faint. The brain wants to block out severe trauma. It may try to put you to sleep. You must not allow it.

I suspect there were elements of the ritual serum that aided in my alertness. At the very least, a diluted amphetamine. Something that made the pain impossible to tune out. An amplifier.

Repetition: Not every night but as often as possible. Repetition increases understanding, reveals new echelons. Repetition shows commitment, drive, ambition, consistency. Repetition allows for patterns to form within the chaos, snowflakes to emerge from snowstorms, breakthroughs, epiphanies. Repetition instills ritual with a spiritual significance. Repetition goes beyond the ritual itself, creating sub rituals. Trips to the drugstore or an emergency room. Applications of ointments, injections of steroids and cortisone and antivenoms and antibiotics. Replacing bloody, puss-crusted bandages with fresh gauze. Giving thanks to The Great Pendulum before falling into dreamless, restorative slumber.

While my rites of passage may sound exotic, pain rituals are ancient and primal. I never complained and I never asked for respite. But while the mind was intact and the spirit was strong, the body began to fail me. Obviously, gloves in public became a necessity. The wounds began to bleed into one another, different bites from different beasts. Various toxins were building up in my fatty tissues. My muscles were shredding, internally. My organs were exhausted with several on the verge of shut down. When my rites were over, when I'd return to The Whole Year Inn where I lived with the derelicts, when my body would at last be allowed to unfurl and revel in its agony, I would wretch and writhe in exquisite misery. Objectively, I knew that I was dying. It was becoming harder and harder to maintain focus. I began to fantasize about piercing the veil.

I was nearing the end of my pre-paid month at The Whole-Year Inn, but there would be no need to pay for another thirty days or even a week. Either my rites of passage would end or I'd die before my time was up. And my time was running out fast.

"I'm a detective."

I met AJ, the detective, in a row of slot machines at The Golden Nugget. My left hand was in a box full of bullet ants. The sting from a bullet ant is considered the most painful in all of the insect kingdom. Each bite feels like being shot, hence their name.

"Oh yeah," I replied to AJ, cool and calm as a bullet ant began to burrow underneath my thumbnail. "Hot on the trail of a fugitive?"

A bit on the nose, perhaps, but I wasn't afraid of a detective or any state or federal authoritarian, for that matter. The investigation into Larry's death had stalled, even though I had been upgraded from a "person of interest" to a legitimate "suspect". They couldn't find me. I didn't tell anyone in California where I was going—where I was really going. I told people I was headed south of Humboldt to join a six-month off-the-grid hunt for Sasquatch. There was a false sighting at Tan Oaks Park in Leggett. Authorities spent a week canvasing the campground and surrounding forests. If I hadn't been selected and guided towards my destiny by The Great Pendulum, I might have enjoyed a six-month hunt for Sasquatch. Sounds exciting, actually.

"Nah," AJ the detective replied nonchalantly. "I'm into some..." he looked over his shoulder to make sure no one was listening, "...deeper stuff."

Dealing with drunks and horny tourists was par for the course on these initiation nights. But AJ was fine. Enjoyable even, which is saying a lot coming from someone with a bullet ant under her thumbnail and another one gnawing on a knuckle. He was clean and handsome even though he appeared to put very little effort into his appearance. His shirt was untucked. His jacket was torn. His hair unkempt and slightly slick like a man who doesn't give a fuck about what people think about him. He could have been in his late twenties. He could have been in his mid-fifties. You just couldn't figure it out.

"Color me tantalized," I replied. "Please, elaborate."

Another bullet ant bit into the webbing between my thumb and index finger. I could feel a few more meandering on my palm, ready to deliver a gunshot blast of pain where I was most sensitive. The suspense was incalculable.

"Oh, I couldn't," was his sly reply. He was nursing a Jack and Coke.

"Well now you're just making me horny. Come on, spill it."

"I'm involved in a lot of things, actually. Most, I couldn't divulge even if I wanted to. A lot of it, though, you wouldn't believe me if I told you."

"Challenge accepted," I said. "Tell me something that I wouldn't possibly believe. Because I'm a pretty open-minded lady." I'd been sent by a pre-cosmic God on a quest to find my Earthly Master, a pain priest with holes in his head, along with a tribe of disciples who all live somewhere underground, after all. Although he would have had no way of knowing that. AJ looked over his shoulder again. "Stop it!" I chastised with a smile. "Tell me!"

"What do you know about..." AJ paused for dramatic effect, "*Ancient Aliens.*"

I rolled my eyes, clearly disappointed. "Damn, I had high hopes for this conversation," I lamented. Though I never seemed to give the matter much thought, I had recently come to the conclusion that extra-terrestrials don't exist. It was something I just knew from the moment I came out of my Death Valley fog. And now it was a certainty. I rejected Zoo theory, the Drake Equation, and the Fermi Paradox without ever having studying them. I considered METI a colossal waste of time. To me, "The Great Silence" was just another one of mankind's feeble attempts to convince themselves that they are not utterly alone. But we are.

"What do you mean?" AJ asked.

"Frankly, I don't believe in aliens, so..." A bullet ant bit the center of my palm. It felt like I'd been crucified.

"Aha," AJ retorted, "I don't believe in aliens either!"

"You're not some 21st Century version of Fox Mulder?"

"That might not be the worst simile, but no. I'm a little more down to earth."

"So why do you want to talk about ancient aliens?"

"No," AJ corrected. "I'm talking about *Ancient Aliens*, the TV show. Have you seen it?" AJ had me on a pendulum swaying between curiosity and disappointment.

"I know that a show exists called *Ancient Aliens*, but no. I've never seen it. Not my cup of tea." The bullet ant under my thumbnail had burrowed down to the bone. The ritual serum of the evening was exceptionally powerful. The room morphed and swirled.

"Well, I've got it on extremely good authority that *Ancient Aliens* isn't what it seems," he revealed.

"You mean it's not a TV show?"

"It is a TV show, but it's not just a TV show." Another long pause. I bit.

"So? What is it?"

"*Ancient Aliens* is a religion."

The rest of the casino faded into the distance as AJ the Detective delivered a passionate dissertation. It wasn't as annoying or absurd as I thought it might be. And while I wasn't sure exactly where my beliefs and his intersected, if anywhere, it certainly made for entertaining verbal intercourse. It was as though the two of us retreated into a void, each of us illuminated by a spotlight. Later, it was as though we were sitting across a table from one another, in our own world. All the while, my hand remained firmly inserted in the bullet ant box.

"They've created a unified theory for everyone and everything: Aliens," AJ began.

"I've seen the meme."

"Of course you have. It was a joke. So tell me: How come the show has been running for eighteen seasons now?"

"Money?" I wagered. But there was really no need for me to answer his questions or even interject at all.

"Money, yes. But also: Brainwashing. Mind control. They've taken the Bible and replaced every interaction with God and Satan and angels and demons with Aliens. Capital A. Then they did the same thing for every other religious scripture. Islam, Hinduism, Buddhism. Chinese dragons for Christ's sake. The Ark of the Covenant was a radioactive piece of Alien technology. But that's just the foundation of Ancient Astronaut Theory.

"Most religions went stagnant a millennia ago," AJ continued, "and that's where *Ancient Aliens* gets insidious. Because it's about more than just religion, isn't it? It's about everything. It's about Aliens helping ancient humans build the pyramids and every other wonder of the pre-historic world. Now you have one explanation that unifies creationism and all of pre-history. What's next?"

"Everything else?" I ventured. I was becoming queasy. Light-headed. Like I was being hypnotized. I feared failing my evening's rite. I struggled to stay connected as AJ the detective continued pontification.

"Exactly! The Industrial Revolution: Aliens. Leonardo DaVinci was an Alien. Nuclear weapons were invented by, and then condemned by Aliens. Einstein was an Alien. The Founding Fathers of America were in allegiance with Aliens. The Presidents know it's true. All the world leaders know it's true. There's an Alien base in Antarctica. Aliens caused the Spanish Flu and COVID. You can use drugs to communicate with Aliens. But it gets worse: Human beings are nothing but a bio-engineered slave race designed to serve Aliens. We've never accomplished anything on our own and we have no power beyond what they have granted us."

"That's some fascinating bullshit," I assured him

"Exactly! And that's not even the craziest part."

"Please," I implored, "do tell me the craziest part."

"The craziest part is that you don't even have to believe in Ancient Astronaut Theory for it to be dangerous. Because soon as the spaceships arrive," AJ made finger quotes around the word "spaceships". "When the spaceships arrive, we'll be pre-programed to bow down, to obey. We'll be triggered, like Manchurian Candidates. Activated."

"Activated for what?"

"Servitude."

"Well," it had been fun, but I was just about ready to go on with my life, my bullet ants. "Good thing we don't believe in Aliens. No chance of those spaceships will ever show up, so nothing to worry about, right? Sounds like a big waste of time and money."

"I never said I don't believe in spaceships," he corrected, again with finger quotes. "I said I don't believe in Aliens, or, more specifically, Extra-Terrestrials."

"So then, where are the spaceships," no finger quotes from me, obviously, "going to come from?"

AJ smiled, wide. He looked down, then back at me. I looked at him blankly for a moment. He looked down again, and this time he pointed at the floor. Then he leaned closer and whispered, "They'll come from underground."

"Oh, wow, okay," I attempted one last time to re-engage. "So, who's flying the spaceships?"

"That's the billion-dollar question right there. All I know for sure is, they won't be from another planet. Because they're already here."

"Well, AJ the Detective," I said as I turned my focus back to my machine. "It's been lovely chatting, but I'd better get back to this slot."

"I know, I know," he threw his arms up. "I said you wouldn't believe me, didn't I?" He was right, I didn't believe him at the time. Or, more accurately, I couldn't. I didn't have the capacity to explore his theories, so deeply invested in my own. When I'd have more time to think, all the time in the world, I'd see things clearly.

"Thank you, really," I said. "I like stories about monsters underground."

His smile froze. His eyes intensified. Something I had said. It triggered him. The word underground. The way I said the word underground. The undertones of longing.

"Wait a minute," AJ the Detective deduced, "you're trying to get there too, aren't you?" Had I betrayed myself, my Underseer, my God? Had I revealed too much with mere intonation? Was this a test? "You've heard about them, haven't you?"

"What?" I asked, feeling exposed and harshly judged.

"Elevators to Hell." I refused to reply and my silence said it all. "Listen, Sybil, I can help you. We can help each other. But we can't talk here." He tossed a matchbook from a greasy diner into my lap, Vickie's Diner on E. Sahara Ave. "Can you meet me here for a late breakfast?"

"I don't know," I replied in a moment of candor.

"Yes," my Underseer said in my earpiece.

"Yes, okay," I told AJ.

"Fantastic. Here's my number." He handed me a business card. "Call or text when you're on your way."

"I will."

"By the way," AJ interjected as he got up to leave. "What's up with your box?"

I had been wise to be weary of AJ, wise to hesitate until given permission to meet him by my Underseer, confirmation that he was indeed a component of my mission. Beyond adherence to etiquette, beyond my impending judgment by The Forlorn Order. Because there were more eyes on me than I realized. And even though I planned to pledge eternal loyalty to my specific tribe and my Earthly Master, it was like Rush Week. And I was being courted by other houses, fraternities with designs not entirely aligned with my own. My movements were being accounted for by some truly wicked forces. I'd have to be vigilant, always on the lookout for signs from The Great Pendulum.

But AJ wasn't a danger. He was a key. One of many. We talked for an hour over scrambled eggs and water, the only things I could hold down after a night with my hand in the bullet ant box. I had been late to meet the detective, in fact. Delayed by my need to scream and vomit in an alley for half an hour. The wrecked, blackened soles of my feet throbbed in solidarity with my hands, my bones, and my gasping organs.

We talked about Disneyland in Los Angeles, of all things. "Did you know that there are dozens of secret doors throughout the park? There are a couple clubs, of course, but also mundane facilities like boiler rooms, storage rooms, break rooms, security rooms... you get the idea. None of these doors are even locked. Know why?"

"No, why?" I asked both engaged and exhausted.

"Because you can't see them."

"Why not?"

"Because you have to know they're there in order to see them."

"Sounds like some Harry Potter fantasy shit if you ask me."

AJ laughed. "You're right. It sounds crazy. But it's true and there's nothing fantastic about it. You know what it is? It's paint."

"Paint?"

"That's right. They used cutting edge stealth technology to create a color called Don't Look Here #42. It fucks with your vision by refracting light. And because you can't see it, your brain fills in the blanks with whatever else is in the vicinity. If the door is on a wall, it will look like a wall. If there's a door on the side of The Matterhorn, it'll looks like the side of a mountain. See what I'm saying?"

"I think so."

AJ wiped egg yolk off his chin and leaned forward. "All the

big casinos have them," he explained. "Elevators to Hell. The trick is knowing which one has your elevator, because you don't want to get in the wrong one, believe me. Once you know where to look, you just have to believe it's there. It'll appear. Eventually. By the way, you're not looking so hot. Are you sick?"

Did I spend days, weeks even, frantically searching every major casino in Las Vegas for secret elevators? Hardly. It was a no brainer, in my case.

I headed straight to the one that looks like a giant needle.

Symposia

When the doors to an Elevator to Hell open, it's like staring out into dead space. It requires a leap of faith to step into that void.

Obviously, I found my elevator in The Stratosphere. I could already imagine it: A shaft at least as deep as the casino is tall, plummeting down from the exact center—like the needle of an antique metal syringe, penetrating deep into the firmament. On the ground floor of the casino, I found a massive pillar where I imagined the eye of the target would be. It was lined with slot machines and ATM machines and monitors and lights. I must have walked around it for hours, drenched and absolutely wretched.

There had been an unusual cloudburst over Vegas when I walked from my meeting with AJ the Detective towards my destiny. A massive thunderstorm that made the afternoon as gloomy as dusk, dumping massive torrents on the bone-dry city. Were it not for a well-publicized network of tunnels and storm drains, casinos up and down The Strip were subject to flooding under such conditions. We all know that these tunnels are populated, primarily by people who want to disappear. For them, days like this must feel like Judgement Day.

"What do you want from me?" I asked AJ before we parted company outside Vickie's Diner on E. Sahara Ave.

"Just maybe keep in touch. Let me know if you hear anything about... you know..." AJ pointed downward.

"*Ancient Aliens*?" I chided.

He raised his finger to his lips and silently shushed me, smiling. "Seriously, let me know if I can help. I'm around."

I turned to walk away.

"By the way," he stopped me. "Where did you say you were from again, Sybil?"

"I didn't"

"That's right," he stroked his chin. "You didn't."

That was when the skies broke open. The city darkened. I hadn't walked ten feet before he called after me again.

"Sybil! Just tell me you didn't have anything to do with that thing up in Sacramento. Tell me that wasn't you."

I smiled, rain running down my forehead and cheeks. A tiny waterfall from my septum ring. "It wasn't me."

AJ the Detective nodded, looking happy and sad at the same time.

I didn't take a car or a taxi to The Stratosphere. I could see it, so I just walked towards it as directly as possible. My hands throbbed. My bones shook. My organs ached. The blacked soles of my feet screamed. My brain kept trying to push me into unconsciousness. But I wouldn't let it. I had set my sites on the beacon, and no rough seas could deter me. It felt like hours. It felt like days. Sometimes, it felt like The Stratosphere was getting farther away the closer I got. My head was bloodied but unbowed. I washed up on its shores, Invictus. Security eyed me as I staggered in, but they didn't stop me.

And after hours of walking around that central pillar, that mighty artery, the cracks began to appear. Some of those ATM machines weren't ATM machines. Some of the slot machines weren't slot machines. Some of the people weren't even people. The harder you looked, the more difficult they became to define. Until I found the keystone, my focal point. I held my gaze, unflinching. And when the doors finally opened before me, the inside of the elevator was black as the pit from pole to pole.

The doors closed as soon as I stepped inside. The lights went on. Polished metal interior, not uncommon for an elevator. No buttons, though. A circular pattern of holes indicated an intercom above a control panel. The control panel contained a telephone receiver connected to the interior by a coiled cord. Then I saw the rectangle, the size of a large hand. I pressed my palm against it, and the Elevator to Hell descended.

I could feel it. That reflexive tightening in my stomach, the lightening of my feet and legs. Going down. There was no display to mark my progress, no way of calculating floors or levels passed. So I started counting. But counting was meaningless. Time was warped, distorting, accelerating, freezing, completely unreliable.

The elevator came to a stop. A siren began to blare. Red lights flashed. The doors opened. Three men in red hazmat suits rushed in and surrounded me. Each carried a wand, connected by a hose to a gas canister on his back. They sprayed me with a combination of chemical solvents, creating a plume of vapor. I coughed and covered my eyes. As quickly as they had arrived, they exited. The doors closed again. The alarm stopped. The red lights ceased. The mist evaporated completely and the descent continued. Faster now.

A bolt of blue lightning shattered my confines and I found myself floating in the presence of The Great Pendulum. I gave awe and drew strength from His divinity. Another deafening crack of shocking electricity and I was back. The scent of afterburn was strong and smoke lingered. The elevator stopped. The doors opened. And I was in the presence of my Underseer.

He spoke my name and I shuddered. "You have been granted temporary access to Terminal Island," he explained. He was smartly dressed in a black suit that looked slightly government issued. "Dr. Oscar Von Knopka has sponsored your petition for asylum." My Underseer wore a strange hat, stylish like a fedora but ceremonial somehow. "We will continue to process the visas necessary for the next leg of your journey." Then he went from bureaucratic to parental. "Come, get off the floor." I hadn't even realized I was folded in a soggy clump at the bottom of the elevator. He helped me to my feet. Then he put his arm around me. "You've done well. And you will be rewarded." I looked up at him, meekly, teary-eyed. "But first," he said with a smile that revealed too many teeth, more teeth than I'd ever seen, "it's time for your processing." Fear. For the first time in weeks, I allowed myself to feel it. The way he said "processing", it was hideous. He laughed. "It'll be much easier for us all if you sleep now." And then he was holding a mask to my face, pumping a sweet mix of oxygen and intoxicants into my gasping lungs. "Sleep..." his voice spun into a feedback loop, echoing, before disappearing into oblivion.

I dreamed about teeth. So many teeth. And then nothing.

And then there was a television set playing a commercial. Something about a breakthrough drug whose side-affects may include a life-threatening infection of the perineum. How long had I been asleep? A dark fog slowly retreated from around the screen until I realized I was back in my stinking room at The Whole Year Inn. I was lying on my bed, still substantially paralyzed following anesthetization.

And I was crushed, of course, finding myself back in this pit above ground. It meant I must have failed. Even after enduring my rites of passage, even after finding my way into the Elevator to Hell. Even after obtaining sponsorship from Dr. Oscar Von Knopka (whatever the fuck that means, whoever the fuck he was), I had been cast out. Denied. Deemed unworthy. I felt worthless. I would have screamed if I could have, so ashamed I imagined I could just die here and rot.

Another commercial, one for generic Viagra, ended and *The Jerry Springer Show* started. But it wasn't *The Jerry Springer show*, or at least not exactly. It looked like Jerry at first, but I'd blink and he'd be Maury, or Montel, or Sally Jessy Raphael. All of them, but none of them. An amalgamation and an imitation. The theme-song blasted, the logo spun, the audience chanted the name of the ever-morphing host.

"Welcome back!" exuded the enthused Jerry-Maury-Raphael. "Today we're talking to fed-up mothers and their out-of-control daughters!" The crowd gushed salaciously as lights came up over a dank stage. There were sets of sad women paired with their insufferable progeny. Cringing, weeping Gen-Xers vs the worst essence of entitled millennials. It was garbage. Nothing I would have been watching voluntarily.

I gasped when I spotted my mother amongst them. Except she wasn't my mother. She was worse, obese, hideous. Her hair had been dyed and unnatural orange. I almost swallowed my tongue when I saw myself sitting beside her.

Except of course it wasn't me. I was a semi-paralyzed heap on a crusty comforter, my head propped up with dirty pillow, going broke and dying from insect torture in The Whole Year Inn while on a mission to appease my God. But there I was. On a nightmarish talk show, looking the most pathetic version of myself I could ever imagine but worse. A plastic, artificial mannequin shell.

"Lois," the host addressed my ogre mother, "what can you tell us about your out-of-control daughter?"

"Oh my God, Phil, I don't know where to begin!" my mom lamented in a voice that wasn't even close to her own. Like a shrill old lady from Queens. "My daughter Darcy..."

"That's not my name anymore!" the TV-me interrupted. "My name is Sybil now!" My voice was impetuous, whiney, revolting. My ugly mother rolled her eyes. The disgusting, increasingly sweaty host rolled his eyes. The crowd booed me.

"My daughter has been driving me crazy since she was a child! I used to catch her in the basement poking herself with needles. She always wanted to play Slap-Face with her friends. She pulled out most of her own baby teeth!"

Montel-Povich-Jones crossed his arms and shook his head, sympathetic to my mother and disappointed by me. "And is it true that things only got worse in her teenage and young adult years?" he asked.

"You don't know the half of it, Oprah!" my un-mother continued. "She became obsessed with horror movies and sex and drugs!" The crowd was becoming unruly. Audience members began turning into human animals. Even the other sad-mother bad-daughter pairs seemed to be united in a disdain for me. "She's pushed me to the brink, Drew! I don't know how much more I can take."

I was in shock. Both as a semi-paralyzed viewer and captive participant in this talk show from Hell.

"It's not true!" TV-me replied in a screeching voice that could pierce eardrums with its annoying tenor. I addressed the host and unnerving audience in rapid succession. "You don't know me! You don't know me!"

Montel-Povich-Jones ignored me. "Lois, what are some of worst things your daughter has done over the years?" The crowd and guests were drooling, bug-eyed, primitive.

"She got into a car accident while driving high!" creature-mother revealed. "She split her face open and almost killed an old couple!" Now, even the camera operators and PAs couldn't restrain their hatred for me. The security guards employed to break up inevitable fights looked like they wanted to kill me. The theater was teetering on the edge of violence. I could feel it.

"It wasn't my fault!" TV-me protested, jumping out of my seat and stomping my feet like a toddler. "They're the ones who ran the red light!" No one was impressed. The volume of angry voices intermingling was becoming intolerable.

"She became a stalker!" my disgusting mother continued. "She almost got arrested in England for following a former actress. Then she almost killed a man in Texas, a writer she had become obsessed with!"

"I wasn't trying to hurt him," I insisted with all the conviction of an infant.

"Those hooks and chains were real, Darcy! What did you think was going to happen to him?"

"My name is Sybil!" I screamed, both on TV and in my nasty bed.

At this point, no one was human. Not the host, the audience, the other guests, my mother or even myself. We weren't animals either. We were puppets. Not cute like Muppets. Vile like Feebles. Each unnatural creation oozed spittle, snot, and slime. Some were sprouting tentacles, others were growing teeth, a few began disemboweling each other.

"And what is your out-of-control daughter up to these days, Lois?" The host was now a four-headed worm.

"She's a fugitive from the law, suspected of murdering her roommate!"

The crowd had heard enough and pandemonium ensued. Chairs flew in all directions. Someone started a fire on stage. Monsters and demons began swinging from the rafters as a pair of hooded executioners wheeled out a guillotine. Cheers erupted, followed by unified chanting: "Kill the bitch! Kill the bitch! Kill the bitch!" I was surrounded and strapped into the contraption. But not face down like you see in the movies. I had been strapped down facing up, looking at the intimidating blade perched above me. "Kill the bitch! Kill the bitch! Kill the bitch!"

"No!" I screamed on television.

"No!" I screamed in my room at The Whole-Year Inn.

The blade dropped. The TV exploded. The walls, floor, and

ceiling were ripped out of existence. And for a while, I could have sworn I'd died.

And then I started to come too again. I was cold. Metal walls. I was back in the elevator. I stood up and realized I was dressed in a hospital gown. How long had I been asleep? I heard the sound of mechanical engagement as the lift started moving again. Moving for certain. But my senses were so scrambled that I couldn't tell if I was moving up or down or sidewise, east, west, north or south. Gravity was out of whack. Where was I going? What had happened while I was unconscious? Should I feel relieved that I was still underground or terrified that I was back in the elevator? Was I headed to a new destination or back to the surface as a reject? Or worse... what if I was being disposed of?

As soon as that thought entered my mind, the elevator stopped with a convulsive clunk. The siren started sounding again. And then the walls started closing in on me. All four of them. The closer they came to crushing me the louder the sirens blared. It wasn't long before I was completely enclosed with barely enough room to turn in a circle. The momentary relief I felt when the walls stopped closing in was dashed when the ceiling started lowering. It was like being in a coffin that was turning into a box. Of course I struggled, pushed with all of my might against this cruel enclosure. I screamed and pleaded and swore and wept. The ceiling stopped before crushing me. There was a short period of unnerving silence. Then a hissing sound followed by a change in pressure. The atmosphere was being sucked out. I could feel the oxygen being pulled from my lungs. More sounds of machinery engaging. Then the floor below my feet began to open. A hot blast shot up at me from below. All I could see was a red inferno as the gap in the floor widened. When the floor had disappeared completely, I had to use my arms and knees to brace myself, to hold myself inside the box. I could have held the position for hours if not for the fact that I was suffocating. Soon I was blacking out, slipping. And then I tumbled into blistering magma, vaporized in an instant.

The pain ended. The fear ended. Everything ended and there was only me.

And then he arrived: My God's Ambassador. My Earthly Master. Hauptnadel.

"There, there, my child," he soothed me. "No need for tears. You are so close to home now. Come. Sit with me a spell. Rest your head in my lap." He spoke with such kindness, touched me with such tenderness, that I melted against him and purred. He continued to soothe me like a child, like his child, stroking my hair, my cheeks, my neck. "We heard your cries all the way from Pavia," my Master told me. "The pain you suffered was so extraordinary, we felt it reverberating from across the ocean. We knew then that you belonged with us." Nothing had been for nothing. "We conspired with an entity to summon you. To lead you to us. To bring you home. And now you are so close."

"Bring me home," I begged. "I'm ready."

"Soon, my child. Soon." Hauptnadel promised. He reached up and removed one of the metal syringes implanted in his forehead. This will help me find you. He injected a mystery liquid into my jugular vein and I sighed with contentedness. As I floated off into a blissful slumber, my Earthly Master promised, "We're coming."

I woke up under a skylight with sunlight on my face. I was in a soft king-sized bed. The bed was in a beautiful resort suite. There were glass doors that led directly onto a white sandy beach. I could hear the waves, feel the salty breeze on my face.

"Good morning," said the man in the corner, sitting in a comfortable recliner. His voice was kind. I rubbed my eyes to see him more clearly. He was a gentleman. He wore an expensive, white day suit. His white hair was perfectly combed. Even his bushy eyebrows looked sculpted, sharp. His tie was violet. His tie-pin was a coin-sized diamond. "I'm Dr. Oscar Von Knopka. Please call me Oz. Please do not call me Dr. Oz."

How long had I been asleep? Long enough to have been transported to a tropical setting. My hands had, for the most part, healed. There was a new pain in my right hand, a new scar on my palm. It was where a new tracking chip had been implanted. Traveling into the domain of The Forlorn Order isn't like visiting another country. Just like entry must be earned through rites of passage, exit privileges must be earned.

"We're so glad you'll be able to join us for the festivities."

"Where are we?" I asked, my throat dry, my voice cracking.

"Terminal Island. Over half a kilometer below the city of Las Vegas. This is my manor. Welcome to Čachtice Castle."

My head was spinning. I looked outside and saw seagulls flying through the sky. "I don't understand."

Oz pulled a slim black remote-control device from his jacket pocket. He pointed it towards the beach and, with the click of a button, the beach became a forest. The temperature cooled and the salt scent in the air was replaced by pine. The seagulls became crows and hawks. A doe and her fawn scampered by.

"We use rooms like this for acclimation," Oz explained. "Processing can be an exhausting ordeal for new arrivals. The realities of life underground can be... overwhelming. Even for those who come here willingly." There it was again. That ugly word: "Processing".

I staggered to my feet and slowly walked towards the glass doors leading "outside". It was incredibly realistic. But the closer I got, the more artificial it became. The depth felt unnatural, movements were subtly pixilated. It was better than any virtual reality game I'd ever seen. But it still couldn't pass for actual reality. Not for very long.

"Would you like to see Terminal Island?" Oz asked me, standing up from his chair.

"Of course," I replied. I wanted nothing more, in fact, than to see where the Hell I actually was.

Oz pointed his remote towards the glass doors leading outside once again. "Outside" disappeared completely. I was looking out of an immense window. My host took me out on the balcony to enjoy the view in all of its maddening enormity.

Video recordings and all forms of photography are forbidden on Terminal Island, as it is not uncommon for celebrities and politicians to visit. Even excessively detailed descriptions of the outpost city are forbidden, for security reasons, so I must tread lightly even now.

It's like a bubble, an immense hollow sphere. Tiers and platforms support all manner of dwellings and industry. Massive architectural wonders are connected by bridges, escalators, and moving platforms. The entire place vibrates with the intoxicating energy of a Moroccan Bazar. The air carried a symphony of voices and machinery. Beneath it all, a constant buzz of electricity, a constant drone from the city-wide oxygen filtration systems. Drones and helicopters dotted the "sky". Terminal Island is a subterranean port, a hub of illegal commerce and excessive debauchery. But for me, at that moment, it could just as easily have been a dystopian spaceship, a renegade station hurtling across galaxies.

Insanely wealthy individuals build insane monuments. Oz's manor was opulent, decadent, lush, and gloomy. He gave me a tour of the south wing.

It quickly became apparent that I was to regard him with the utmost respect, as he literally held my entire future in his hand. He spoke almost constantly while guiding me over multiple acres across multiple levels, each one buzzing with activity. People were chattering about the upcoming "festivities".

First, we discussed logistics and protocols. In addition to being a port and a playground destination, Terminal Island houses the judicial and legislative branches of The Forlorn

Order. Access is tightly controlled, as the outpost's mere existence is a tightly guarded secret. All invitations must be pre-approved, and not just for those coming to Terminal Island as a final destination, but anyone desiring passage to or through any domain governed by The Forlorn Order. The entirety of the organization's territory was called The Real Estate. The near endless subterranean expanses beyond the control of The Forlorn Order are known as The Frontier(s). Communities that settle there no longer receive the protection of The Forlorn Order. And they are no longer bound by their rules.

They Acolytes of Ascension had recently relocated to an abandoned region at the borders of The Frontier(s), an area called Akrimonium. Once established, Hauptnadel declared sovereign independence while taking control of and repurposing much of The Forlorn Order's existing infrastructure. It caused a rift, one that had yet to be ameliorated to the satisfaction of all parties. My invitation had come directly for Akrimonium, without pre-approval, and The Forlorn Order was claiming a breach of protocols. The way Oz explained everything was much more complex and detailed. Frankly, tedious. Beyond my bailiwick. All I cared about was finding my tribe and my Earthly Master.

To that end, Oz explained that I was to serve out a probationary period under his observation and tutelage. Once my loyalty and psychological constitution has been confirmed, the good Dr. would approve my visa and help to arrange my transport to The Frontier(s). "Don't look so glum," he told me as we sat on a veranda, sipping a sweet, psychedelic brew. "I suspect you'll be on your way before too long."

As for how he knew my Earthly Master, Oz explained, "He and I were part of the same secret society. One with ancient roots. A congregation of radical, revolutionary thinkers seeking to push the boundaries of science, art, and technology past all conventional understanding. We call ourselves The Kōmos: Men and women capable of reshaping the course of society in dramatic, unimaginable ways. Utopians, nihilists, and spiritualists. Your 'Earthly Master' and I had overlapping interests, especially in the areas of accelerated human evolution, chemical explorations, and paraphilia. We believed that true breakthroughs exist in the extremes, that ancient urges connect us to our past and our future. We are both proponents of transhumanism. Your 'Earthly Master' is a truly gifted pioneer. But, like all great minds, we clashed and went our separate ways. Disagreements over methodology, for the most part. Nothing too dramatic," Oz assured me.

As for the festivities everyone at Čachtice Castle had been buzzing about: "The timing of your arrival could not have been more perfect," Oz beamed. "Tonight, you'll join me for Symposia. Tomorrow, you'll be my guest at a very special wedding. Expect your time here to be legendary!"

It would be. Legendarily fantastic. Legendarily disastrous.

The tradition of Symposia was first established by the ancient Greeks, leading to epic tales of extravagant feasts and hedonistic orgies. While adhering to the established rituals associated with Symposia, Oz's gathering was unique—an event I could never have imagined. It seemed like a large percentage of the permanent residents of Terminal Island were in attendance, along with scores of visitors. Several thousand in total. They filled many rooms and several tiers of Čachtice Castle. Many of them wore masks. The dress code was impossible to establish. There were as many people in formal wear as there were attendees completely naked along with every conceivable style in between. Acrobats and clowns created mayhem in every corner. Interactive art installations spewed smoke, fire, and lasers. Rows of tables were covered with delectable delicacies, many of them served on the hairless bodies of beautiful young men and women. I assumed they were alive because of how healthy they all looked. But none of them ever moved a muscle or even blinked.

I found one of the party's many intoxication stations. Imagine a bar with every known brand of alcohol along with unlimited quantities of high-quality drugs. If the number of options is overwhelming, a server will make you something exotic. Martinis tainted with ayahuasca, lemon drops with ketamine, amphetamine-infused Long Island Iced Tea. Hallucinogens and dissociative abounded, and it wasn't long before I was caught beneath the landslide, gliding through rooms, across dance floors, up and down stairwells, and through sex dungeons—all under the watchful eye of my host, the illustrious Dr. Oscar Von Knopka.

"I can't wait to introduce you to my wives," Oz whispered into my ear.

"How many wives do you have?" I asked.

"Fourteen."

A bell began to toll and guests started filing into the Castle's amphitheater for Carnivale. I took my seat near the front row. Now, as a resident of Northern California for the majority of my life, I'd seen some incredible variety shows. And I don't just mean entertaining. I mean transgressive, dangerous, probably illegal. Sacramento's Scream Queens, for example, are epic, pioneers of "Gorlesque". As for the most notorious show in the Bay Area, I'd attended Tourette's Without Regrets at the Oakland Metro at least thirty times over the years. But what I witnessed during Carnivale that night was unlike anything I'd seen, more spectacular than any Vegas Circus or apocalyptic wasteland. More depraved than anything I might have previously shuddered to dream.

I'd seen suspension before. I'd even practiced suspension. But only a few times. While I found the pain exquisite, I didn't receive the same high many others spoke of; a feeling of being free, liberated, flying. Quite the contrary, when my flesh had stretched to its limit, when my body left the ground by hook and chain, I felt significantly tethered. Like an animal on a leash. But the suspension demonstrations I saw that night were extravagant. Bodies attached to elaborate apparatuses, spun at great speeds and then inverted, hoisted on wires in unison to create gravity defying ballets. Blood and sweat dripped over the audience like rain.

One man took the stage alone to perform a feat of endurance and suffering. A spotlight bore down on his thin body, dressed only in a loin cloth. A lone hook on a single chain slowly lowered from above. The man pierced his tongue with the hook, then held his arms out in the crucifixion pose as the chain was pulled back up. He was pulled off the ground. And he hung like that, twenty feet above the stage as the crowd roared. It wasn't too long before his tongue began to stretch to an unfathomable length. Blood gushing, the man never lost a modicum of poise. Eventually, you could see a huge hole forming below the piercing, as the tough muscle began to split. Then, with a tremendous ripping sound, the man fell back onto the stage. His tongue, all the way down to the root, remained on the hook, swaying under the spotlight.

Oz leaned over and whispered, "He's an artist and a spiritualist. Tonight's performance coincides with a lifetime vow of silence."

The artist took a triumphant bow, blood gushing from his mouth, grinning with glee. He received an eighteen-minute standing ovation.

Carnivale was so much more than acts of suspense and suffering. For hours, insane musical ensembles, uncanny contortionists, hip-hop wordsmiths, acrobats, comedians, performance artists, dancers, and illusionists all took the stage, all pushed their niche talents to transcendent extremes that both shocked and fascinated. Of course, things began to take a darker turn after the human sacrifice. Darker, but just as vivacious.

For the final act of Carnivale, a performer surgically removed his own kidney through his navel. Without pausing, or even seeming affected, he cooked it over a stovetop that had been wheeled on stage. For twenty minutes, he prepared his dish with the intricate attention of a gourmet chef, all the while gushing blood from his abdomen. Those of us close enough could smell the meat as it sizzled, enhanced with shallots and red wine. When it had been plated and set to perfection, the artist sat down at a table with his organ and, under the light of an ornate candelabra, he ate it.

"Autophagia," Oz explained.

If I hadn't suspected it when I'd woken up that morning, there was no denying it now. Terminal City is teeming with cannibals.

The Wedding

Spontaneous acts of cannibalism continued throughout the remainder of the evening and into the morning hours.

Yes, there are morning hours in the underground city known as Terminal Island. They keep the same hours as the surface world, for consistency's sake. During the "day" the top half of the massive sphere is illuminated. An artificial sun rises in the east and sets in the west, creating brilliant displays at both ends, fiery patterns across a blue sky dotted with artificial clouds and holographic birds. At "night", the "sky" darkens and a glorious digital moon waxes and wanes in unison with its actual counterpart outside. Stars and galaxies swirl and mesmerize.

"At least half of visitors to Terminal Island come for the cannibalism," Oz informed me over breakfast. We ate morsels and drank psychedelic tea at a banquet table. "That's why you were vaccinated against prion disease during your processing." Remnants of the evening's debauchery were everywhere, including guests who were passed out (or deceased) in just about every corner and alcove. "It's the original taboo, the line that separates us from animals and insects." In addition to his activities with The Kōmos, Oz had been a psychiatrist before relocating to Čachtice Castle semi-permanently in 2011. "Would it surprise you to learn that the desire to commit hedonistic cannibalism naturally increases in proportion to a person's wealth?"

I hadn't slept since awakening in Terminal Island. Between the unusual anxiety, intoxicating formulas, and shocking activities I'd witnessed, I could barely close my eyes.

Regarding this evening's wedding: "I've known the Bride and Groom for years," Oz explained. "I introduced them. So, I'm especially honored to be hosting their ritual union."

As a private practitioner and Senior Professor at the National University of Natural Medicine in Portland, Oregon, Dr. Oscar Von Knopka specialized in the study of Body Integrity Identity Disorder, or BIID. Body Integrity Identity Disorder, aka Body Identity Dysphoria, aka Amputee Identity Disorder, aka Xenomelia (or Foreign Limb Syndrome) is the desire to be disabled or the feeling of discomfort about being able-bodied.

"I had patients who wanted to amputate otherwise healthy limbs," Oz explained. "A few also wished to go blind or deaf.

"My colleagues, afflicted with limited imaginations, obviously considered BIID a condition to be cured," Oz continued. "They invented something called Cognitive Mismaping Theory, a disconnect in the sensory cortex of the parietal lobe of the brain that detects somatosensory information coming from the arms, legs, and face. They suggested factors like childhood trauma, obsessive compulsive tendencies, and exposure to amputees at a young age. They sought to treat this so-called disorder with drugs and cognitive therapy.

"But I believed something quite the contrary: That those with BIID weren't sufferers or victims in the slightest. Similar to gender dysphoria, they wish to exchange their able body for an incomplete one. They are, in fact, Transable, responding to a primal urge, something genetically encoded. They believe a part of their body does not belong to them. I was the first to ask, 'Well, what if they're right?' I asked my colleagues, 'What if we encourage these men and women to fulfill their desires by employing the services of qualified surgeons?' I was nearly ostracized. Accused of turning my back on the Hippocratic Oath."

After breakfast, we continued our conversation strolling through the castle's exotic arboretum. "You've heard the theory that losing one sense heightens another, haven't you Sybil?"

"Of course."

"And do you believe it's true?"

"Well, I once saw something on YouTube about a blind kid who taught himself echolocation." Recounting this now, it feels almost like foreshadowing. "He could ride a bike and even play basketball."

Oz was delighted. "That's a marvelous example. So, what do you think happens to a person who loses a limb?"

"Well, you hear about soldiers who've lost limbs talking about phantom pain."

"Intelligent. Yes, that's a proven phenomenon. But it only occurs to those who were comfortable in their original, whole body. What do you imagine would happen to someone with BIID who lost a limb, a part of their body that they had always felt didn't actually belong to them? Do you think it could similarly lead to heightened sensitivity in the remaining limbs?"

"I certainly don't see why not."

"I had my own theories. I proposed the Transable could unlock new neural pathways by dissociating themselves from unwanted body parts. More incredible, I suspected that the Transable could eventually become completely Transphysical, thereby laying an important stepping stone towards the next stage of human evolution. An evolution in consciousness. Well, can you imagine how may colleagues reacted?"

I shook my head. I couldn't.

"Let's just say that I wouldn't be getting any University funding for my research. That's when I brought my studies to The Kōmos. For a time, your 'Earthly Master' was a consummate collaborator."

I had been tolerating Oz's pontifications to the best of my ability. He was, after all, my sponsor, my host, my advocate, and a cannibal. But his work, and the way he was making sense out of something so bizarre, was genuinely fascinating. And now that his tales included my Earthly Master, even in periphery, I was rapt.

It was past noon by this point in our conversations. The artificial sun was high and bright in the "sky" above Terminal Island as we meandered through Oz's extensive hedge maze. "Transableism was surging in the 21st Century, a mystery no one could explain it at the time. Like any misunderstood and persecuted community, they were forced into hiding. Seeking solace in backrooms and basements. Poor souls packing their limbs in dry ice, laying themselves over railroad tracks, traveling thousands of miles to meet disreputable doctors for inadequate results. Lost in the shadows, shamed into secrecy, hoping to find respite in drugs and therapy but, of course, never finding any. Such a travesty." As we walked, Oz and I smoked extra-long cannabis cigars peppered with psilocybin.

"I gave the Transable respect, reverence," the good Doctor continued. "We gave them the best care and attention possible, as medical professionals and empathetic souls. We cleared qualified candidates for surgery and, within a month, we touted a 70% success rate. 70%! That's beyond what any drug or methodology would have dreamed of. All by simply removing unwanted biological matter, the same way an oncologist removes a tumor. No more anxiety or depression for 70% of our study participants!" Oz was clearly proud of this accomplishment. "Still, it wasn't enough. We wanted 100%!

"That's when we began to incorporate my flair for the artistic with your 'Earthly Master's' penchant for ritual and spirituality. We took our studies out of clinics and hospitals, re-establishing sessions in theaters and art spaces. We turned amputations into ceremony, incorporating artists, shamans, and cutting-edge machinery. We added music, drama, and spectacle. Invitation only events became immensely popular. Eventually, we had to find larger venues. We created a community much larger than the Transable alone. We sparked something that resonated with misunderstood mavericks and so-called degenerates from around the world. Allies. We noticed an especially strong bond forming between the Transable and a community of consensual cannibals. It wasn't long before our amputation ceremonies were followed by feasts, where the fresh, donated meat would be consumed.

"To be clear, my study of and attraction to cannibalism has nothing to do with survival." It was now afternoon and Oz and I were enjoying a light lunch by the castle's grotto. A motley crew of overnight guests were holding an impromptu orgy in the swimming pool as our conversation continued. "The survivors of flight 571 who crashed in the Andes, the Donner Party, those set adrift on The Raft of Medusa—they didn't have a choice. Cannibalism ceases to be a paraphilia when survival is at stake. Humans are hard wired for it. When I talk about cannibalism, I'm talking about an ongoing psychological need. A desire to acquire attributes of another through consumption. A desire to obtain collective consciousness.

"I'm appalled by unethical cannibalism, to be perfectly frank," Oz maintained. "You can find long-pig fajitas down in the slums of Terminal Island if that's what you desire. Unethically harvested, disease-ridden specimens pulled from encampments on the outskirts, butchered in bacteria-infested backrooms before being shipped through sewers. Obviously, I consider such callousness deplorable."

"Absolutely," I agreed.

"The Forlorn Order has no official stance on the practice, allowing each estate to maintain their own regulations. Rest assured, all acts of human consumption at Čachtice Castle are consensual and symbiotic. Moreover, we've given the practice inextricable tenets designed to advance our physical and perceptive capabilities. Let me back up for a moment."

After a swim and a shower, Oz gave me a tour of the aviary, introducing me to his favorite exotic birds in between his dissertations. "We decided, your 'Earthly Master' and I, that the time had come to establish a new society, a sub-sect of The Kōmos. A collective of minds looking to explore the intersection of Transhumanism and Collective Consciousness. We dubbed ourselves Contingentiam, The Contingency. We chose the Conjoined Twin as a mascot, believing its symbolism and subtexts to be multi-layered. As a metaphor for the Transabled, each twin is encumbered by body parts that are not their own. For those driven to seeking attribute absorption through consumption, the twins represent assimilation and assembly—the zygote of an eventual hive, a human society with the telepathy and analytic execution of insects.

"Those were glorious years," Oz beamed in a state of unabashedly nostalgia. The late afternoon found us in one of the castles many gaming rooms. Not playing pool or cards or Russian Roulette as many of his guests were. Simply lounging on immaculate leather couches, sipping pipes loaded with opium and MDMA. "Our gatherings were extraordinary. Not the caliber of last night or what you'll experience this evening, but tremendous nonetheless. We'd bring dozens, sometimes hundreds together under the Conjoined-Twins insignia. Near equal numbers of the Transable and ethical consumers in an effort to create the perfect balance of psychic energy. We designed a special communion that became the ritual centerpiece of our gatherings.

"One giver, one receiver," Oz explained. "Brought together on a stage that would become an altar. Officiated over by philosophers and musicians. The giver would donate. The receiver would assimilate. The giver would offer a limb. At the very least a hand, an eye, or the tongue. It would be extracted by a crimson surgeon and a hooded occultist. Sometimes the removal would be fluid and precise, a single slash from an immense pendulum or specially designed guillotine, for example. Sometimes the removal would be blunt and brutal, carried out with mundane tools or even scraps of stone, glass, or metal. The receiver, compelled by compulsion or the same longings that spurned the Aztecs and secret elite military ranks from before history all the way through the Pacific theater of World War II—the receiver eats. They may choose to eat the flesh raw or cooked to exacting specificity. All souls present will chant a persistent mantra until a glorious climax of pyrotechnics and nitrous oxide.

"And then," Oz continued in his state of blissful remembrance, "After the games and the dancing, the long drinks and the long walks... Then, I assure you, Sybil, the real fun begins."

The afternoon was getting late. The artificial sun had nearly completed its calculated arc across the dome and the "sky" above Terminal Island had transitioned into a moody purple. The wedding was set to begin in a few short hours. "The met at a Contingentiam retreat in Aspen," Oz explained of the evening's key players. "The Contessa Bohumila Jovanović and Viscount Rasvan Mostafa. They make a beautiful pair but, more importantly, they represent the future. Neither adheres to the traditional boundaries of a husband or a wife. Likewise, as members of The Contingency, neither one can be considered strictly a giver or a receiver. They are Transparaphetic!"

"What does that mean?"

"It means that their wedding will include elaborate

pageantry, arcane trials and metaphysical interludes. The participants and the audience will be tested, both physically and mentally. And when the demonic summonings have concluded and the interlopers have been condemned, when their names have been recorded in the Chronicles of Lazarus, then Contessa Bohumila Jovanović and Viscount Rasvan Mostafa will eat each other."

I thought I saw my God's Harbinger a couple of different times at the reception. "Where has he been?" I wondered, realizing I hadn't seen him at all since arriving in Las Vegas. Was it really him? I couldn't have known for sure. Not only was my brain swirling from a celebratory combination of intoxicants, but the crowd was mammoth, nearly twice the size of the previous evening's Symposia. At a party this size, in a place like Terminal Island, there's bound to be more than one attendee in an S&M mask with rabbit ears.

The ceremony had been every bit the gorgeous bloodbath Oz had predicted. Now, the betrothed sat elevated at a table of honor. Crimson surgeons performed the amputations. Their attendants saw to the couple, providing drug cocktails necessary to keep the Contessa and Viscount conscious and voracious. Chefs prepared the meat at immaculate cooking stations that had been assembled by their sides, providing the freshest cuts for mutual consumption. At one point, an occultist removed the Viscounts gallbladder with his fingertips, placing the steaming organ on a bed of arugula. A sous-chef grated a truffle over it. The Contessa ate it in a single mouthful. The Viscount playfully smeared a drop of blood across her face. The crowd roared boisterously at the loving displays, which continued until they both lost too much blood to continue. Before they retired to the master suite for a ritualistic evening of assisted sexual intercourse, Oz pulled me aside.

"My wives and I would like you to join us for a private supper in a more intimate setting."

"Of course," I replied, as if it would have been possible for me to respond otherwise.

"One of my attendants will summon you at midnight."

Everything I had seen and experienced since arriving at Čachtice Castle had me in a state of perpetual awe. I was excited and constantly mesmerized by splendor and grotesquery. But I was also feeling confused and conflicted with increasing levels of dread and foreboding. I couldn't wait to continue my pilgrimage, to finally meet my Earthly Master face-to-face, to join my tribe. But I wasn't in a hurry to leave Terminal Island, even though a voice in the back of my head suggested I should be.

Oz wanted me to meet his wives. All fourteen of them. Should I be honored by my host's offer? Should I look forward to basking in the company of fourteen beautiful and intelligent women? What kind of intellectual, sophisticated women would the Doctor choose as his life-mates? Did they spend their days and nights engaging in otherworldly delights?

And what was Oz's ultimate interest in me? Was he merely my platonic sponsor? A respected philosopher and administrator who had taken me under his protective wing, offered me shelter in his opulent estate? Was there an unspoken agenda? Was he grooming me? Did he want to fuck me?

Did I want to fuck him?

When the heavy, somber bells struck twelve times, most of the guests said their goodbyes and began filing out of the castle. I, on the other hand, was escorted to Oz's personal quarters by a pair of albino twin butlers. While Oz had taken me on hours of tours over my two days in his care, there were still massive portions of his estate that remained unseen, and were therefore unfamiliar to me. I was guided over a series of staircases, ferried through secret elevators hidden behind bookcases, and down a long, dank tunnel that felt unnaturally cold. We arrived at a mighty set of double doors, wooded and immense. Each butler swung a side open, and I was directed inside. No sooner had I stepped in than the doors swung closed again. A *woosh*, a slam, and the sound of a mechanical mechanism locking.

Oz's personal quarters displayed the all opulence of modern royalty tempered against the macabre sensibilities of a 16th Century vampire. A vast opened space with stone walls and vaulted ceilings adorned with crystal chandeliers. A mini-inferno rage in the fireplace with the ferocity of a small volcano. The entire chamber pulsed with a psychedelic overtone, either by design or owing to my personal levels of adrenaline, exotic intoxicants, and sleep deprivation. A dusky gloom put everything slightly out of focus. Tunnel vision threatened to invade my periphery.

There was an elaborate dining table set for three. One of Oz's wives was already seated. She was exactly the stunning, sophisticated woman I imagined. Poised, classical, almost statuesque. Oz was relaxing a few yards away on his quadruple King-sized bed, a glorious realm of sensuality surrounded by four elaborately carved posts and a velvet canopy. The Doctor had unfastened his bow-tie, along with the top buttons of his shirt. White, dignified tufts of hair pushed out from his chest. He was smoking a cigar while lounging amongst a pile of beautiful cushions, stroking one of them lovingly as though admiring its craftsmanship and quality. He seemed to be whispering something, chuckling, as though reliving a recent conversation.

He collected himself upon my arrival, straightening his shirt and cummerbund before greeting me at the doorway. "Sybil, you look divine," Oz told me, taking my hands into his before leaning in to kiss my cheek. "I'd like you to meet my wife, Athena," he said gesturing to the woman at the dining table. "We're so pleased you could join us."

"Nice to meet you, Athena," I said with a flippant wave that must have appeared crass. I cringed inside. Athena didn't reply, but she smiled and hummed softly, sweetly.

"Please, have a seat."

The table could have seated at least a dozen comfortably—which makes sense for a man with fourteen wives. Though why was there only one at the table so far, I wondered. Where were the other thirteen? Oz sat at the head, of course, his back to the crackling fireplace. Athena was sitting at his left. I was seated directly across from her on Oz's right. Her gaze was captivating, engaging. She continued to hum pleasantly, a girlish, satisfied sigh, at regular intervals. Servers appeared from behind a pillar insinuating a secret kitchen connected to the quarters. There would have to be, considering how far we were from the castle's hub. Wonderful aromas filled the air as plates of painstakingly prepared morsels were placed around us. Mussels, clams, oysters, and one gigantic crab leg, at least the size of a baseball bat, intimidating pincher still intact, threatening to snap back to life.

Oz whispered to one of his servers who left and quickly returned with three stone goblets, each containing a potent, thick red liquid.

"A toast!" Oz exclaimed. "To you, Sybil. May you realize all of your heart's desires." What was it? A combination of infected dog's blood, manchineel sap, and research chemicals, perhaps? At this point, it hardly mattered. We lifted our glasses and drank deeply. Athena seemed to have a bit of trouble lifting her glass. It seemed to take longer for her to extend her arm, concentration to bring it towards her lips.

"We've been very impressed by your temperament, Sybil."

Athena hummed a note of agreement.

"Not everyone who visits is able to maintain your composure," Oz continued. "You seem comfortable, even in the midst of insanity. Not everyone survives their first Symposia."

"Thank you." It was true. I hadn't become outwardly shocked or appalled by any of the transgressions I'd seen, even when I was disturbed and disgusted. For the most part, there was simply too much wonder to behold.

"You should be pleased to know that I've approved your petition for semi-permanent relocation. Your final visas should be ready in just a few more days.

"Amazing! Thank you!" I gushed.

"Of course, we'll be sad to see you go," Oz said.

Athena hummed in agreement.

"You've been a wonderful host. I can't thank you enough."

"It's a shame, actually. Athena agrees that you exhibit amazing potential, perhaps more than anyone who's ever graced this estate. We'd love for you to become part of our community. We think you would be happy here."

I wasn't psychic yet. I had yet to acquire my telepathic abilities. But I'd been asked to be part of threesomes dozens of times, so I new it was coming. But there was something else Oz was carefully attempting to propose—something just as intimate but much more urgent than sex.

"Oh, wow. Oz, I'm touched. Really. You have a wonderful community and I'll never forget the things you've shown me. But I've made... other commitments." The Great Pendulum had called to me. My tribe was waiting for me.

"Have you? or were those merely the circumstances that brought you here, to your actual destiny?" Oz stood up, looked into the fire, and spoke with authority and precision. "Do you think this is all I do here? Host parties? Eat flesh and fuck?"

"Of course not!" I replied, fearing I'd already nicked his ego. But the truth was, I had no idea what Oz did when he wasn't hosting Symposia or ceremonial unions. I'd only known him for a weekend. I hadn't given the slightest thought to how he occupied the bulk of his time beyond a life of extravagant riches and extreme sensations.

"I'm at the center of a truly revolutionary movement," Oz assured me, "one whose mission is universal!" He turned to face me. "You think you've seen everything at Čachtice Castle? We have research centers and laboratories, professors, scientists, and engineers. We're finding cures for diseases. We're unlocking the secrets of the mind! The world is about to change forever, and we will be at the forefront of a new age, a new Renaissance. And you, Sybil, we believe that you have an important part to play. Perhaps even the most important part of all." The Doctor was fraught with passion. I was both exhilarated and intimidated. "You're so-called 'Earthly Master', that Hauptnadel—he's nothing but a parasite! He must not be allowed to waste your abilities on frivolity!"

Blasphemy! But at the time, in that moment, I was suddenly incapable of rational thought. And I was enthralled. Great Pendulum forgive me, but the Doctor's passion was infectious. His words implied a brave new world, a sacred world, with a spot of prominence carved out just for me. Temptation overwhelmed me. Pride pried inside me. Surely a man with the seemingly unlimited power and resources the Doctor wielded could deliver on his promises, no matter how outlandish.

"You belong with us," Oz insisted. "We need you."

"Why me?" I struggled to comprehend, even as my ego swelled. "Why do you need me? What makes me special?"

"We've seen your feet."

Athena hummed a note of confirmation.

It was time for the main course.

"This beautiful woman sitting across from you," Oz said, gesturing towards Athena, "She's more than just my wife. She's the embodiment of my work. They all are."

A team of servers removed the uneaten Hors d'oeuvre and set out a covered platter. Even covered, the entrée smelled amazing. Simultaneously, two crimson surgeons emerged from the shadows and began disassembling the Doctor's wife.

Her chair had wheels. They pulled her away from the table and removed her prosthetic feet and shins, placing them on the table beside the platter and accompanying side dishes.

Oz stated the obvious: "She's Transable. All of my wives are."

One surgeon removed Athena's left arm at the shoulder, an elaborate prosthetic constructed from cutting-edge polymers resulting in a completely natural looking appendage. The other surgeon removed the glove on Athena's right hand, revealing she only had two digits left: Her thumb and middle finger. It made her arm look like a fleshy, alien version of the giant crab leg we'd just consumed. Athena's claw, while much smaller, was much more terrifying.

"She's a giver. All my wives are."

The surgeons removed Athena's dress. She had no breasts. Her ribs were glaring, her gut sunken, abdomen crisscrossed with scars, tubing emerged from her navel before disappearing into an apparatus beneath her wheelchair.

"Tonight," Oz stated emphatically, "you and I will both be her receivers."

One of the surgeons removed portions of Athena's face. Latex cheeks, an artificial chin, glass eyes. She only had half a tongue. The vocalizations I had mistaken for hums were actually coming from a ventilator pumping oxygen into her single lung at regular intervals.

"I've been saving her thighs and ass for as long as possible," Oz explained. "Those parts are the tastiest!" Though bandaged, I noticed blood dripping from a recent flesh extraction below Athena's hip. In that instant, a server pulled the cover off the platter revealing the savoriest, most well-prepared cut of rump ever cooked. Juicy, seasoned, perfection. "But tonight is a special occasion."

A slice of Athena's ass was placed on a plate in front of me, doused in a teaspoon of yellow sauce. And though I was ravenous, this moment necessitated a pause. Though opportunities had already presented themselves, I had not partaken in any forms of human consumption at Čachtice

Castle. But I wasn't plagued by ingrained morality either. Consensually donated meat is objectively more ethical than factory farming. Still, there was a symbolic stumbling block threatening to trip me up. The realization that eating human flesh would make me an eternal outsider within society. But I was already an outsider, wasn't I? I didn't have any plans to return to Sacramento or anyplace above ground, did I? I was already damned, wasn't I?

Athena opened her mouth and, with great effort, managed to croak: "Eat me."

And so I did. I ate Athena. I let Oz cut small pieces on my plate. I let him feed them to me like a child. And when I swallowed, it was as if a new chorus of voices began stirring inside me.

"This is not an ordinary meal," Oz assured me. "This is assimilation. Do you feel it?"

"Yes," I whispered, my eyes nearly rolling into the back of my head.

"We're connected now," Oz continued as he fed himself. "The three of us. We'll always be with you." A trio of violinists emerged from the shadows to serenade us until the meal was fully consumed.

"And now," Oz said with a smile that was both a gift and a trap, "It's time for dessert."

The servers, the surgeons, the musicians and random attendants all disappeared into the shadows. Oz led me towards his bed. Athena remained seated at the table, "humming" in approval, occasionally cackling softly. The Doctor swept me off my feet and laid me down amongst the cushions. The entire bed seemed to tremble with anticipation, as if the mattress were somehow alive.

What choice did I have? Could I have refused? Run screaming from Čachtice Castle? Made my way through the thoroughfares of Terminal Island? Clawed my way back to the surface despondent and dejected? Did I want to leave? Leave this palace of earthly and otherworldly delights? Leave this community of freaks and free thinkers? Leave this room, this bed with its promise of carnal catharsis? Was I in control or merely a passenger to a destiny much larger than I had previously imagined?

Oz removed his shirt, revealing a Conjoined-Twins tattoo on his chest. "We're so happy to have you with us this evening. All of us."

I smiled before it all began to click. "All of us?" I asked, looking around the room and seeing only Oz and Athena.

"All of us," Oz repeated. "Myself and all of my wives." His wives. Since the first hour I'd met the Doctor, he'd been mentioning his wives. All fourteen of them. So why had I only been introduced to Athena? Where were the rest of them?

"Will any of them be joining us tonight?" I asked in a daze of meat, drugs, and lust.

"Oh, my dear," Oz said, amused. "They're all right here."

Something on the bed was moving. Slithering. Chattering. Something in the cushions. No. It was the cushions themselves. Moving, as though awakening, rocking back and forth. They weren't cushions. They were his wives. They weren't wrapped in pillowcases; these were their evening dresses. And now they were beginning to strip. "Here's Beatrice and Catherine," Oz introduced as heads began emerging. "This is Heidi. That's Clementine. Over there is Alexandrea." Soon they were all naked.

Each woman had been whittled down to her physical minimum after years of donating flesh to Oz. Each head was little more than a skull wrapped in skin, eye sockets empty and gaping. Each had a thin neck stripped of muscles and tendons connected to a rattling ribcage. "There's Vanessa and Christina. Here's Stephanie and Ophelia." Each wife had a single arm, practically stripped down to the bone, capped by two digits:

Their thumbs and forefingers. Just enough to push a button, lift a glass of wine, or pinch. None of them had any legs, not even stumps.

Even their abdomens had been robbed, with only remnants of organs remaining, just enough to survive. Most were connected to lithium battery packs that powered pace-makers, ventilators, and feeding tubes. "This is Consuela, this is Emerald, and this is Lyric." The wives began squirming, moaning, pulling themselves around us with their "claws", their heads dragging on necks unable to support their weight. "And this lovely lady is my first wife, the woman who made me what I am today: Amanda."

Amanda opened her mouth and spoke in a small voice, like a kitten crying for attention: "Never more in love."

I finally noticed that each wife had a perfect vagina. Oz was still having sex with them. Even those who no longer had a pelvis had vaginas. Fully functional, excited, glistening vaginas. Some waxed bare, some with pristinely manicured pubic hair, some with copious bush, some pierced. Thirteen vaginas cuddling against me--and another one at the table. Athena was masturbating, rocking back and forth, grunting. Imagining what she could not see.

Oz held a psychic connection with them all, having consumed enough of their flesh to allow for a transfer of consciousness. He doesn't hold a piece of them, or a combination of attribute. He holds them all inside of him. They communicated, conspired, and moved in coordinated unison, like bees.

As Oz's body pressed down on top of me, his wives caressed me with their claw-fingers. I felt one probing my inner thigh as another attempted to enter my mouth. They touched me everywhere. "We are one," Oz moaned as he reached down to remove his penis from his pants. Athena, not wanting to be left out of the action, had thrown herself on the floor and was now pulling herself towards the bed, cackling, pulling a trail of tubes and wires behind her.

"I want your eyes!" Oz exclaimed as he prepared to enter me. "I want to eat your rods and cones. I want your gray jelly!" I spread my legs, tilted my hips upward, and arched my back, preparing to be enveloped in this pile of living corpses, pulled into a sexual assimilation by a cannibal, the doors exploded open.

My God's Harbinger ran inside, exchanging gunfire with a team of bodyguards in the adjoining corridor. The wives screamed and scattered, most of them finding shelter under the bed. Oz leapt to the floor in a state of shocked perplexity. Alarms went off. A female computer voice announced an "Intruder Alert" over the intercom.

"Don't believe a word he told you, Sybil!" my God's Harbinger commanded. "He's not a leader or a scientist or a philosopher. He isn't even an artist!"

"What's happening?" I asked, I screamed.

"Dr. Oscar Von Knopka," my God's Harbinger yelled. "He's an Acrotomophile! He's just a fucking fetishist!" As pandemonium raged, my God's Harbinger removed his mask and told me, "My name is Mortimer Nada and I'm here to rescue you! Come with me if you want to live."

Arrival of the Acolyte

Bells were ringing and unseen angels were singing as the door of the subterranean cathedral swung open.

"Welcome home, my child." It was my Master, the man with the metal syringes in his forehead, beckoning me. "We are so happy to see you." His smile was Paradise. He held his arms open, inviting me into an embrace. The Acolytes of Ascension, my tribe, revealed themselves behind him. They surrounded us, enclosed us, creating an orb of pure healing bliss. I wept.

He looked amazing, my Master. Bright and transcendent. His ceremonial robes, though worn thin over years of use, gave him a sacred aura. The Acolytes: Beyond merely beautiful, beyond merely shocking, a kaleidoscope of twisted flesh, punctured faces. And smiles.

I surely made for a rude juxtaposition, dressed in tatters, layered in filth, rife with parasites and diseases. My hair, now matted, now white, hung in clumps that ran past the black soles of my gangrenous feet.

It had been forty years since I had escaped from Terminal Island. Forty years of climbing through caves and shafts, shimmying through pipes and vents like a rat. Forty years of scavenging for insects and their casings, my manna from Heaven. Forty years of sucking water off of rocks, crawling down drains, and decaying. I'd been serving time: Forty years of wandering the hostile and desolate Frontier(s). Forty years of torment. My crime was worshiping false idols.

Every Jew knows the story, even the very young ones, even the unborn ones. God sent Moses to Egypt to liberate the Israelites. God parted the Red Sea and Moses lead the Children of Israel out of slavery. But when Moses left them alone to commune with God on Mt. Sinai, the Jews panicked. Fearing the futures uncertainties, they resurrected a pagan demigod and held it hostage inside a golden calf. In a moment of weakness, they turned their back on God, committing bloody sacrilege. As penance, God ordained that the Children of Israel would wander the deserts for forty years before finding the Promised Land. And even though Moses had nothing to do with the uprising, he was punished as well. God ordained that his ambassador would never set foot in Jerusalem.

The Great Pendulum sent me Moses in the form of his Harbinger, sent him to lead me to the promised land. But in a moment of weakness, I'd been seduced by a charlatan, a wealthy monstrosity who turned a personal amputee fetish into a false religion. I wasn't being punished because I almost had sex with Oz and his menagerie of meat puppets. I was being punished for believing his lies, imagining myself his new Queen, willing to dismember myself for his approval, a devotee of his delirious dogma. It was the moment that I tilted my hips upward that doomed me. That universal motion of consent was interpreted as a grave sin.

Oh, how he taunted me relentlessness, Dr. Oscar Von Knopka, that manipulator, every day, every step of my forty-year struggle.

"You'll never escape us, Sybil," Oz's voice would boom

directly into my head. His wife Athena hummed in agreement. "You ate her meat. Now we live inside you. Forever." I'd bash my head against rocks, but his voice stalked me even into unconsciousness. "You could have been my wife. My Queen. The center of a vast Transphysical network. Intercontinental. Interplanetary. All I wanted was to eat your eyes. And your arm, your left one. And your legs. And your breasts. Your tongue. Your remaining muscles and connective tissues. Your organs, as many as you can spare without malfunctioning..." For hours, for days, for decades. "We're already aligning with powerful forces. Wheels are turning. Rome will fall and a new age will begin! An age where men and women are unencumbered by their physical constraints, free of gravity. A cybernetic age of quantum mechanics and witchcraft! We will put the whole world to sleep!"

"Leave me alone!" I'd scream into darkness. "Go fuck your pussy bags!"

And I admit it. Over forty years, I couldn't help but second guess myself. I pondered the life I could have had. Even being shaved down to a pillow-sized monstrosity with genitals might have been preferable to the loneliness, the hardship, and the hunger. I replayed the most dazzling and captivating moments of Symposia, imagining myself an integral part of the circus. I dreamed of endless celebrations with paraphiliacs and madmen. But that's what got me into trouble in the first place, isn't it? Second guessing. Daring to believe that I knew better than The Great Pendulum, that I could choose my destiny.

Regret is the King of all the demons, smashing jealously, revenge, and greed into pulp. Regret, not just for my betrayal, but for everything. I thought about Larry for the first time since before I arrived in Terminal Island. He had been so easy to forget amid the art and chaos of Čachtice Castle. But I thought about him during my years in the bowels of the earth, and as more than just a satirical stereotype. I thought about his parents. Larry had parents. Just because I had never met them doesn't mean that they didn't exist. Of course they did. And now, they were suffering. Just like my mother was suffering, and maybe even my dad, wherever he might be. Regret, not just for the pain I caused to those closest to me, but for the suffering I wrought on strangers. All of it. Regret possessed me, ravaged me, left me wrecked and shredded. But it wouldn't kill me. Killing me would have been an act of mercy.

In an effort to console myself, I tried to imagine those who had it worse than me. Those children in Austria, locked away in a secret room beneath the basement by their father who was also their grandfather, left in a stinking dungeon for twenty years with their mother who was also their sister. Or the Faizrakhmanists in Tatarstan, the cult of twenty men and thirty children who lived in an eight-level underground compound beneath their mosque, where they claimed independence for both Russian Law and orthodox Islam. Thirty children, born underground, and the oldest at twenty-seven was hardly a child anymore. All that time spent in dug-out rooms without ventilation. I imagined I was one of them. And worse.

As a child and teenager, I was obsessed with the Chowchilla mass kidnapping of 1976. I hadn't even been born yet, and I didn't know anyone involved, but from the first time I heard about a bus full of kids who were buried alive, my world shattered. I knew for certain that I lived on a planet inhabited by monsters, despite everything my mother had told me.

Before the internet and true crime on demand, exact details were hard to come by. So I'd let my imagination fill in the blanks. I imagined the kidnappers, surrounding the bus, pushing their way on board, holding the children hostage. And I was one of them, the children. And we were driven somewhere to be buried alive. At my youngest, it seemed most likely that they were buried at a cemetery, because that's where people were buried. I had no concept of ransom at first. It never occurred to me that the kidnappers planned on giving them back. Burying them alive seemed so absolute. So final. I imagined the kidnappers had dug a huge grave, and they lowered the bus into it on a platform like the ones they use to lower coffins—whatever that contraption is. And then they covered them with dirt, committing an act of absolute terror certain to make them famous in the Annals of Evil.

Of course I had always known that they'd been rescued. I imagined the cops rolling in to save the day the way they always did on television and in the movies. But that didn't change the fact that it happened, that a bus full of kids was buried alive, that this was the world we lived in and monsters are real.

The thing about the Chowchilla mass kidnapping is that it actually becomes more terrifying when you know all of the details. The events that transpired on July 15, 1976 were beyond what my unbridled childish imagination could have possibly conjured.

The basics were all as I had imagined. Frank Edward "Ed" Ray has driving twenty-six students back home following an afternoon field trip to a local public swimming pool. At around 4 PM, a van blocking the road forced him to bring the bus to a halt. James Schoenfeld, Richard Schoenfeld, and Frederick Newhall Woods IV jumped out of the van, each brandishing a firearm, each wearing pantyhose over their face. It was a trap. Now here's where the details begin to elevate a terrifying situation even worse. The Devil is in these details.

One of the gunmen drove the school bus, one held a firearm to Ray's head, and the third followed behind in the van. But they quickly ditched the bus in a washout along the Chowchilla River. Since it wouldn't be long before the kids were reported missing, they covered the bus and loaded Ray and the kids into a pair of black vans that didn't have any windows. Now that they were in disguise, the kidnappers drove their captives around for over eleven hours. Imagine the sick anticipation they must have felt, not knowing where they were going. Not knowing what was going to happen.

They eventually arrived at a rock quarry in Livermore, a place owned by Woods' father. They had pre-buried a box truck in the side of an embankment. They were transferred from the vans and into the truck through a hole on the roof of the cargo hold. Then they sealed the opening. Then they used a tractor to load fresh dirt over the top of the hole, making the truck and its occupants completely invisible. You might agree that these details enhance the true horror of this event and, believe me, it gets worse.

Down in the truck, Ray and the kids found mattresses, water bottles, and snacks. They found that the truck had been fixed with a ventilation system, something that was both a relief and downer. While the two fans ensured they wouldn't suffocate, they, along with the crude "toilets" cut into a wheel-well, suggested the captives might be stuck for a long, long time. Can you imagine, because I imagined. I imagined myself with them, crying, screaming, retching—a ten-year-old coming to grips with mortality.

Unbelievably, the kidnappers couldn't get ahold the Chowchilla police in order to relay their demands. The lines were tied up for hours by parents, worried community members, and media reporters. They finally decided to give up and, after a long day of kidnapping and false imprisonment, they decided to call it a night. They all drank beers, got drunk, and fell asleep.

But while the kidnappers may have been enjoying a moment of calm, the captives in the box truck battling bedlam. First one of the fans stopped working. Ray and some of the older children wondered if one would be enough to sustain them indefinitely. Then the other fan stopped working and they knew that none of them would survive the night. The temperature had risen significantly in the hours since the captives had first descended, and the walls of the truck were becoming wet with condensation. The air was hot, becoming acrid. They'd have to fix the fans or they'd be dead by dawn. Then the roof started collapsing.

The weight of the earth on top was more than the frame of the box truck could bare and it began to buckle, folding in on itself. It happened in fits that suggested they'd be crushed in a matter of hours. No one was coming for them, not the kidnappers or the police or their parents or fucking Batman. They were going to die—unless they did something themselves.

Ray and the older kids stacked mattresses until fourteen-year-old Michael Marshall was able to reach the opening they'd been lowered down through. He was hopeful that he could tunnel out. But the kidnappers hadn't just covered the top with a metal sheet, they weighted it down with a couple of hundred-pound industrial batteries, a fact that was no doubt contributing to the trucks current collapse. Still, through sheer strength and determination, no doubt fueled by unprecedented levels of adrenaline production, Marshall managed to slide the metal sheet to one side, creating a passageway he could only barely squeeze through.

But the nightmare wasn't over. Marshalls weight on the roof only seemed to accelerate the gradual flattening. Worse, the fourteen-year-old now found that the kidnappers had constructed a wooden box around the opening in the trucks roof—and it was locked from the outside. Like the final protagonist in a horror movie, there was new terror, new depravity at every turn, no guarantee that making it this far would ensure success. Imagine Marshall's frustration and rage. Imagine how he must have felt, baring the totality of fear produced by the children at death's door below him. Imagine how hard he must have kicked against that box. Hard enough to break metal. Certainly hard enough to shatter wood. And that's what happened. A few more inches of earth, and Marshall was free.

Soon, they were all free. Sixteen hours after being buried alive, Ray, Marshall, and the rest of the captives were free. But it must have felt like so much longer. It probably felt like forty years. These and other thoughts occupied my time, ameliorated my suffering, helped me to imagine light at the end of a near-infinite tunnel.

I dug like a victim of premature burial gasping for air. And I swam and I squirmed and I jumped into holes. Passed the last constructed corridors of The Real Estate, beyond the realm of The Forlorn Order. Into the lawless, perilous Frontier(s) teeming with undocumented beasts of every phylum, marauders of misery. And after forty years, I'd seen it all. Everything ever written about life underground in all the books in all the world. And more. The secrets of the Elders and their untapped powers, I'd seen it. Even AJ's ancient aliens: Seen. I roused sleeping giants, toppled mighty tyrants, and took a ride through the belly of the beast.

Oh, the stories I could tell them, my Earthly Master and my tribe, surrounding me in a singular loving embrace. How I could regale and entertain them with details of my voyages. if only my mind was still intact. If only I could still speak or express myself at all without grunting and screaming. If only I hadn't lost every shred of my humanity.

My toenails and fingernails had grown into twisted yellow branches stained with tar. My hair was infested with insects and even a litter of small animals. I had chewed my tongue out in a fit of insanity during my twenty-fifth year of penance. I pulled my ears off my head in a futile effort to silence Oz's infernal degradations. My skin: Bleached leather covered in scabs and boils, dripping with puss, draped loosely over my bones. My bones, riddled with hairline fractures and brittle with osteoporosis, grinding into sand with every motion.

After forty years in a metaphorical desert, I had finally arrived at my Promised Land just in time to die.

Even though they survived, Ray, Marshall, and all of the self-rescuers of the Chowchilla kidnapping were and are forever haunted by their experiences. It was too much for them to endure. And even though I had bested every so-called god and monster the underworld could summon, my body was too broken to enjoy any rewards. My mind, snapped and rewired, pulsating with impending aneurisms, no longer able to comprehend the riddles of true enlightenment. Still, I had arrived. And I was finally an Acolyte.

"It's such a shame," my Earthly Master lamented as he brought me into the ceremonial bathing chamber. "So much has changed since you've been away." My tribe laid me down into a tub of black stone. Pitchers of warm, perfumed water were poured over me. My disgusting, greasy locks were shorn, my nails removed with tools. I was dried by the softest towels and dressed in a robe denoting purity and dignity. And still, I was a crone, a hag, completely decimated. A terror to behold.

"Things could have been much different, I think, had you arrived in time." The cathedral and its alcoves were in a state of disrepair and neglect. The red-hot fires that had fueled fierce orgies during times of celebration has long cooled into embers. And even though my Earthly Master and the Acolytes looked physically and spiritually vibrant, the pervasive sorrow made it clear that this was a dying tribe. How old was he now? Over one-hundred? "We think that you may have been the key." A tear, a goddamn tear stained my Earthly Master's cheek, bringing with it the full impact of my treachery. My failure had somehow led to this impending demise. "Because now, it's too late. It's too late."

Like a bride being walked down the aisle by a proud father, my Earthly Master took me into the last room I would ever enter, a grand chamber my dying eyes struggled to interpret. A laboratory, a theater, an auditorium—all of them and something very different. The architecture was alien, geometric and insectile, unlike anything that had existed before my exile. The air tasted artificial and sinister, a subtle green light emanating from the corners, pale blue light emanating from a singular source above. Everything started coming into focus.

In the center of the room was my coffin. A daunting box, elevated into a position of prominence below the light source. A glorious altar atop an altar. It dripped with cables at all ends and in between, cables that were also vines and tentacles, twitching and spitting green sparks form exposed pores. The tendrils crossed the floors and connected to the walls, climbed up them, burrowed into them. The walls that accepted these oozing cables flashed with lights and displays that blinked like eyes. The entire room vibrated with the hum of finely-tuned machinery, but also groaned and whispered in its recesses, like a pack of hunting animals.

After forty years of digging through mud, I had emerged into an era where technology wasn't created out of raw materials in factory. It's grown organically in labs, birthed into living components that throb and shimmer like fresh meat. There had been a synthesis, a conjunction, a turning point that made all of history before it insignificant. I wouldn't live to comprehend it.

"In spite of all the turmoil and trauma, we managed to carve out a lovely corner of Hell for ourselves. But this new world," my Earthly Master lamented, "I'm afraid it's not for the likes of you, dear Sybil." He walked me toward the apparatus of my dispatch. "And so now is the time for us to say goodbye."

A glass lid slid open and I was helped inside the wondrous box. And as I took my final repose, the Acolytes filed by in a processional, laying wreath of paper flowers and pagan dolls made out of bones and string at my sides. The love I felt was overwhelming. How I wished to express my gratitude for their acceptance, however brief. Unseen angels began to sing from an unknown dimension in an unknown language. Finally, my

Earthly Master stood over me. "It's such a shame," he said, "that you won't remember any of this when you leave us."

"Yes I will," I replied with my eyes, "I'll remember everything."

"No, you won't." It was definitive.

The glass lid closed. My Earthly Master and the Acolytes took positions all around me. Dozens of cords with mouths like lampreys emerged from interior panels of my coffin. They dug into my limbs and my abdomen. I didn't fight them. A silver worm slid up my nose and began delivering soothing toxins directly into my liquified brain. The coffin began to fill with a thick, pink liquid, much thicker than water. In a matter of moments, I was completely immersed, suspended in an acidic aspic.

My master pulled a great lever and the skylight above me opened. A great blue light illuminated the room. Bolts of lightning burst into spider webs above us. Even this far beneath the earth, my Earthly Master pulls electricity from the atmosphere! Amazing! Small fires broke out in every corner. Green sparks rained and living machinery hissed.

"Sybil." My Earthly Master's voice sounded clear through a built-in intercom, or perhaps directly into my brain. "What do you suppose is the secret of time travel?"

I had no idea. Except, in that moment, I knew exactly. If I wasn't encased in jelly on the edge of oblivion, if I still had a tongue to speak with, we might have said it in unison.

"Pain."

My Earthly Master engaged a switch. Sirens wailed and walls began to crumble. A blinding white light consumed me. A bolt of blue lightning smashed into my coffin—and there it was. For the first time since my night in Pavia, I reached a new threshold, a new level of suffering I could not have previously imagined, a new high point beyond the highest point. A state of plasmal and cellular agony that simply cannot be communicated. I heard bells tolling. I imagined the scent of burnt ozone. And then there was nothing.

Then an apocalyptic cacophony as I found myself in the presence of The Great Pendulum. I basked in glory as air rocketed into my lungs, nutrients surged into my veins, liquid flesh hardening like wax, bones regenerating. Like an arachnid shedding exoskeleton, the crone was subtracted, my penance was retracted. Another soul-shaking crack of blue lightning. The acrid taste of afterburn.

I was back at Čachtice Castle, Oz stuffing his dick back into his pants. Wives were using their unnerving, singular pincher arms in pathetic attempts to pull themselves under tables and into corners. Athena thrashed so hard on the floor her feeding tube came loose, squirting a repugnant sludge. Mortimer Nada was at the door, emptying clips on unseen teams of bodyguards rushing in to rescue Oz.

"He's an Acrotomophile! He's just a fucking fetishist!"

I was startled, confused, disoriented. I felt as though something profound had transpired, like I'd just woken up after being asleep for days with a vivid nightmare slipping through my fingers, slipping into nothingness.

"Don't listen to him, Sybil!" Oz protested. "We have to deal with these radical fundamentalists from time to time. A byproduct of Terminal Island's liberal immigration policies I'm afraid."

A stream of bodyguards burst in from a secret door behind the bed. Nada pulled a new semi-automatic from his waistband and leveled them in a line. Bullet ridden, they fell in a pile.

"Sybil!" Nada protested, "We don't have time for this. You know who I am. You know who I represent. You know what's on the line!"

I ran to him.

"Sybil!" Oz screamed, his face reddening, his hair a mess. "You have no idea what you'll be sacrificing if you leave this palace!" He was incensed, incendiary, trembling with wrath and abandon.

"Fuck you! Fuck you and your pussy-bags!"

Between waves of guards, Nada used a small device to blast a hole in the floor, revealing a tight, winding staircase. As Oz raged and his pillow-woman croaked and wept like frogs and kittens and babies, Nada pulled me into the castle's catacombs.

An unprecedented surge of adrenaline led to an abysmal crash and, eventually, my legs gave out below me. Above us, the continuing sounds of chaos, Oz ordering his goons to apprehend us or die. The Harbinger knelt down to pick me up.

"My name is Mortimer Nada..."

"I know your name," I assured him. "I'm coming with you because I want to live."

"Listen, Sybil, it's not safe for us to stop right now. Not until I get you out of Terminal Island. Dr. Von Knopka holds too much sway here. If they catch us, we'll never get out again."

"I understand," I told Nada, gasping, nearly hyperventilating. "But I need you to do something for me."

"What?" Nada replied.

"Hit me."

"What?" Nada replied again, this time confused.

"Hit me! I need it!" I pushed my chin towards him, begging for a crack across the jaw or eye.

"What?" Now he was getting annoyed. "Sybil, we don't..."

"Hit me and we can go!" Finally, frustrated, Nada hit me. "Again!" I demanded.

"Sybil!"

"Again!" I screamed. Nada hit me again and then, without me even asking, he hit me again. My God, how I needed that. Like a blast of cocaine obliterating the cobwebs, delivering clarity. "Thank you," I told him as I got back on my feet. "Thank you," I said as I dried my eyes and wiped my nose, setting my constitution for the battle at hand. "Let's go!"

"Yeah, don't mention it," Nada responded, leading me deeper into the catacombs.

Terminal Island is a cesspool. Like the city of Las Vegas above it, it commoditizes sin, thriving on all of mankind's basest instincts, offering the illusion of refuge to those who no longer wish to play by society's rules. "What happens in Vegas stays in Vegas" is only true because we agree it's true. But since Terminal Island doesn't even technically exist, it's a paradise for the discerning hedonist, seemingly free of repercussions. A haven for supposedly dead celebrities, old-money billionaires, and millionaires with connections. And of course, their guests. They're fresh meat. And let's never forget that it takes a city of service workers to keep this neon underworld humming, worker-bees scurrying behind the scenes. Like Sodom and Gomorrah combined, set adrift in international waters, hidden by an artificial hurricane and forces harness from the Bermuda Triangle. Like an island. Like Pleasure Island in *Pinocchio*.

But Terminal Island is also a filter. The unbridled, uninhibited playground may appear like a final destination for the elite seeking to dine on human flesh, hunt human prey, or hug the walls of blood orgies. It may seem like an oasis for artist and revolutionaries for whom "dropping out" was only step one. But it's also designed to contain. The sex fiends, the extreme occultists, the financial assassins, radical scientists, the unyielding spiritualists, the utopians and the nihilists are mesmerized by the never-ending delights. They forget that Terminal Island is just a hub. A station. A starting point. The center of a fist that represents the boundaries of The Forlorn Order's control.

Dr. Oscar Von Knopka is one of many extremely rich white men who have castles in the exclusive hills of Terminal Island. Each castle holds its own horrors. And splendors. For just as the rich enjoy privileges the poor can only dream of, the elite of the elite can create islands within islands. Tribes within tribes. Those with enough money can live in a perfect world of their own design where anyone daring to disturb the illusion can be shot and eaten. Even these power-mad absolutists don't have the desire to travel deep into the web, past the last outposts and the abandoned societies, into the untamed and fertile valleys of the Frontier(s). Frankly, they haven't got the guts to explore this land of shock and trauma.

You'd have to be crazy to want to travel beyond The Real Estate, right? Exactly. Crazy enough to leave it all behind. Crazy enough to believe in a vision you had one night at a sex club. Crazy enough to endure weeks of insect torture. Crazy enough to break bread with cannibals. Crazy enough to follow a man in a gimps mask with rabbit ears through pipes and shafts, down cliffs and over chasms. Crazy enough to march into Hell on shredded feet that, even after all these years, continued to drip tiny streams of blood and ink.

"You'll have to wait here for The Boatman," Nada told me, leaving me on a landing at the edge of an actual cesspool."

"Are you kidding me?"

"They'll be watching all of the official corridors. It's the only way to get you inside the Frontier(s). Once he drops you off, just use that map I gave you."

"Got it right here," I said, holding the folded paper up in my hands.

"I'm going to double back, make sure none of Dr. Von Knopka's cronies are still trailing us."

"Will I ever see you again?" I asked in a moment of shameful sentimentality.

"Not likely, Sybil. You and I are on different paths."

And with that, Mortimer Nada, my God's Harbinger donned his gimp-bunny mask and hopped off into the darkness, down another rabbit hole.

The Boatman arrived a while later. He demanded a fingernail and my two front teeth for passage. It was easy money. I couldn't have been happier to get sailing. I was so close at last to my Earthly Master, my tribe, my homecoming. I smiled so wide, blood gushing over my bottom lip, down my chin, dripping into the feted waters. Propelled onward by the foul-scented mariner across this disgusting bog, clouds of gas bursting into red and purple plumes, hovering above the water like Will-o'-the-wisp, guiding our path, we sailed on.

And when I arrived at the gates of the cathedral I was glowing, proud, hysterical. I rang the bells and the doors swung open.

"Welcome home, my child." It was my Earthly Master, the man with the metal syringes in his forehead, beckoning me. "We are so happy to finally meet you." Finally! Yes, but was it? Hadn't we met before in the astral realm? If we had, he wasn't revealing it. Not yet. But what did it matter? I was home!

He opened his arms, beckoning me. But unbelievably, I froze. My Earthly Master, he looked different than I had imagined. It was obviously him; it was Haupnadle. He was less a God and more a man than I imagined, but that's expected when meeting one's idols.

It was his hands. I'd never seen them before. Not physically. I'd seen his beautiful face, his unique modifications, but not his hands. I had only imagined them, caressing me. Now I was seeing them, actually seeing them for the first time.

Each of his fingers, including his thumbs, was capped with an antique metal syringe. They glistened under the lights. Drops gathered at the needles' tips like diamonds. The fingers of each hand were connected by tubes and wires to a pair of apparatuses on his wrists. It was a startling sight and I was stunned.

"Come to me," my Earthly Master commanded. "Come to me." And I did. And as I fell into his arms, he penetrated me, ten times with ten needles.

And to think. I hesitated.

Transformation

In late 1960, John Lennon suggested he, Paul MacCartney, George Harrison, and Ringo Starr participate in a trepanation ritual as a group activity. And while Paul and the boys weren't savvy, John was apparently committed to the idea. The man he employed to carry out the procedure, however, refused after examining the "Imagine" songwriter. The man believed that John's skull had never completely fused, that an opening already existed, that his Third Eye was already active.

After a stint with Ken Kesey and Timothy Leary on a converted school bus traveling the United States, my Earthly Master became a disciple of Bart Huges, a discredited Dutch Doctor, LSD advocate, and proponent of trepanning. Huges believed that the procedure immediately increases blood flow to the brain, allowing for an equalization of blood and cerebral spinal fluid, an imbalance that's existed since early man first began to walk erect. The result: An elimination of "stagnant pools" of fluids. The potential: Eradication of conditions like dementia and Alzheimer's. He was so certain of the treatment's potential he performed a self-trepanning, in public, with a dental drill. When he went to the hospital for an x-ray to prove the procedure had been successful, he was locked-up in a psychiatric ward for three weeks.

Trepanning, also known as trepanation, trephination, or trephining, refers to the surgical process of boring a hole in the skull, wide enough and deep enough to view the dura mater, the milky membrane encasing the brain. Trepanning is the oldest known form of surgery, and it's still practiced regularly to this day, although only for targeted pressure relief, and with the ultimate goal of replacing the missing piece.

In 1968, Kara Merrill underwent trepanning to alleviate a life-threatening condition. And while she noticed an immediate relief from anxiety and surge in creativity, she attributed the changes to an improvement in overall outlook following the success of her surgery. Ultimately, she elected to have the removed portion of skull replaced. When she healed, she felt less carefree, less energized than she had before. She regretted her decision.

Everything I know about trepanning I learned during the indoctrination portion of my Cadet Phase with The Acolytes of Ascension. We studied the banned, supposedly "lost" documentary *Heartbeat in the Brain* by English drug policy reformer Amanda Feilding, briefly released in 1970, like it was gospel. Her self-trepanning, recorded by her partner Joey Mellen (who would go on to document his own self-trepanning process in the book *Bore Hole*), is considered an original sacrament, the selfless work of a modern-day saint.

Even after a newborn's skull fuses, a layer of fluid remains around the brain until early childhood. This is why children are more receptive to the unknown, possibly paranormal activities. But by the time a body hits puberty, the cranium has completely encased the brain, creating a constant pressure. Trepanning releases the brain from its calcium cage, allowing it to float, facilitating a return to the child-mind state. The benefits are extraordinary.

"This is just a taste of what awaits you," my Master told me as he zeroed in on his target. In tribute to Huges courage, he treated worthy Cadets to a re-enactment using the very same dental drill, a treasured antique he spared no cost to acquire. The bit tore through the skin on my forehead in an instant. Then I felt it pushing hard against my cranium. The pressure was so intense I could smell myself burning. It broke through to my dura mater with a pop that was shocking. The pop was followed by a *schlurp* and a surge, as though my skull was gasping. And when I could feel it, my heartbeat in my brain, I was saturated in a cooling ecstasy. Once my training was complete, my official, ritual trepanning would serve as my final rite of passage, my baptism, my rebirth.

The first real trepanning opens a bore hole just big enough to accommodate one of my Earthly Master's sizable syringes. But the goal is to slowly widen the portal to something about the size of a quarter. Some Acolytes have taken it even further, pushing the structural integrity of their skulls in an effort to free their frontal lobes. We cover our portals with custom caps or glass globes to prevent infection, but ritualistically remove them to allow for the insertion of my Earthly Master's needles. So specific is his understanding of the human brain, he can pinpoint the perfect spot for specific injections. He knows exactly where to find the precious pineal gland. When he hits it, and the potion is perfect, ascension is a certainty. True ascension simply cannot be achieved without undergoing the process of ritualistic, surgical trepanning. This is our belief.

10% of all skulls recovered from the neolithic era show evidence of trepanning. It was clearly a common practice even though, during this era, the survival rate was less than 40%. But that would change over the centuries. Evidence of trepanning has been found at archeological sites in Europe, North and South America, and East Africa. They've even documented evidence of the practice in China where the Eastern culture has long leaned towards herbal and nonsurgical medicines. Hippocrates gave specific directions on the procedure from its evolution through the Greek Age, at which time the survival rate was an astonishing 90%.

Yes, trepanning was done for medical reasons, the relief of pressure following trauma, the removal of bone fragments, and whatnot. But it was just as often a ritualistic remedy, designed to exorcise metaphorical and literal demons. Archeologists exuviating an ancient Magyars' graveyard in Hungary discovered almost 20% of the population had undergone trepanning. They were the wealthiest, most respected members of their community, and many of them had undergone the procedure on multiple occasions. Clearly, they held strong to the belief that trepanning was a key to unlocking psychic potential, specifically clairvoyance.

So why did the widespread, intercontinental practice of trepanning abruptly recede into the darkest corners of history, like a dirty secret? Archeologists in Hungary concluded this custom's disappearance coincided with the Magyars' conversion to Christianity. It's just another example of an evil, organized religion outlawing the mystic. It's especially ironic since, as my Earthly Master contends, "Jesus Christ clearly had a hole in his head." He says so with complete sincerity.

The Acolytes of Ascension are, obviously, a secret society. I know that the term has lost a lot of meaning when the Freemasons are idolized in Hollywood, when the annual atrocities performed at The Grove are common knowledge, when hooded devotees gather beneath the statue of Shiva the Destroyer at CERN, when the Knights of the Solar Temple hold youth recruitment drives. Still, you won't find any leaked footage from our domain on YouTube, no Reddit threads baring our initials, and we intend to keep it that way.

We are not a cult. We are a non-proselytizing, non-denominational, semi-closed community, a congregation dedicated to manifesting the visions of my Earthly Master. Many of our rituals and beliefs are too sacred to share. Our holy documents and relics are locked in impenetrable boxes. And while there is no law against me documenting these reflections, I'm primarily compelled to address misconceptions. Specifically, the lies and slander spewed by that lost soul, that pathetic, unworthy cadet in the throes of withdrawal, that human earthworm who said that I molested him.

I fucking hate him.

My Earthly Master speaks in a variety of accents. It's a way of paying tribute to his mentors and channeling psychic energies. And, yes, he has a flare for the dramatic, a trait no doubt inspired, even if unconsciously, by his years of collaboration with Dr. Von Knopka. He's fond of the German persona: The power, the energy, the ability to terrorize. It's not a disguise. It's a design.

Hauptnadel isn't even his name. It's his rank, signifying his position as our Earthly Master, the personification of our unique crucifix, the downward pointing needle!

The Acolytes of Ascension reside in an abandoned, unincorporated, disputed corner of The Real Estate, an area we consider part of The Frontier(s). I can't give you any surface landmarks, coordinates, or depth to orient you or grant perspective. I couldn't even if I wanted to. I have no idea. All I know is it's deeper than Terminal Island—a lot deeper. Deeper than anything I had previously imagined. Deeper than I ever imagined it would be possible to live and thrive. So deep, darkness lost all of its meaning against the physical, liminal constants of earth and air.

it's impossible to establish a viable community of any size in this region without immense wealth. Luckily, my Earthly Master comes from a family of great prosperity and power. I cannot confirm or deny any speculation regarding his identity or lineage. And while our compound is modest when compared to the insanity of Čachtice Castle, the affluence required to manifest our sanctuary is evident. There is a grand aesthetic that matches our collective energies, adorned with extreme effigies and priceless exhibits.

We have a Cathedral, complete with bells that echo treacherously throughout the cavers of the underworld. We have rooms for congregation, for consumption, fornication. We have labs and operating theaters and a library. There are secret places where fires burn, where transmissions are sent and received, where, once in a moment of quiet dread, I heard a baby crying. The lower levels, where we keep the cadets, are dark and gruesome. It's a test of endurance, you see. They must earn their way to the upper levels. Or else they must leave.

The Acolytes of Ascension are a semi-regimented collective of individuals dedicated to exploring the extremes of sensory perception in an effort to accelerate the next phase of human evolution. We believe it will be a mental evolution. That while inextricably bound to the physical body, human consciousness will be able to travel to other worlds, maybe even other dimensions.

To that end, each Acolyte is encouraged to fashion their body into a conduit, to perform sacraments in the form of ritualistic transformations. Newly inducted Acolytes begin their preliminary transformations as soon as the skin heals from around their trepanning portal, when one begins to receive visions of their true form, when their secondary sensory abilities begin to manifest.

We are monastic in this approach.

Body modification, at its most basic, is vanity. A desire to beautify, stylize, accessorize. Those who become devotees understand, or at least sense, the transhumanist aspects of the practice. They're drawn by a primal desire to enhance the human body. But modification is only the first phase of transformation.

The Acolyte named Sebastian was drawn to ancient practice of tattooing, as I was when I went on my pilgrimage to Pavia, in what seemed like a previous life. His body is completely covered except for the palms of his hands and the soles of his feet. No one knows or can guess what his original skin pigment was. Now, he offers services to Acolytes also seeking to turn their bodies into a living talisman. On the surface, in his previous life, he was a tattoo artist by trade. Now, in our underground sanctuary, he is the Tattoo Master, a prince of the vibrating needles. Find Sebastian if you want to incorporate blackout or sacred geometry into your essence, sigils or incantations, symbols or hieroglyphics.

Surface modifications, tattoos and scarification, are hardly the only options available to the committed, transforming Acolyte. Piercing is popular, though we take the practice to extremes that would be considered abnormal, shocking, even repulsive in so-called civilized societies. The Acolyte named Zoe is a princess of the puncture, able to twist metal and alloys through flesh, muscles, even organs and bones. Needles and spikes, gemmed mosaics, hooks, windows, and horns are all available for implantation. But there's more.

We have doctors, biologists, and chemists for gender transformations and amalgamations. The Acolyte named Bellatrix, for example, became a hermaphrodite. And these collaborators continue to push boundaries. It won't be long before an Acolyte will be able to request a second, or even a third penis or vagina. Beyond gender, these collaborators experiment with adding tails, fins, retractable teeth and claws—even wings. Everything bio-engineered and harvested in the compound's laboratories. But there's more, because if you can dream it, you can be it.

A subset of Acolytes are dedicated to exploring flayed skin as a sustainable sacrament. The beauty of the flayed form and the intensity of pain the practice bestows have always been measured against the inevitable mortality it causes. Those who are flayed don't live long. Even those who are only partially flayed usually succumb to infections in a matter of weeks. But how glorious would it be if we Acolytes could shed our skin and continue to live and thrive? Not wounded, but enhanced, a veritable beacon of sensation. And so this subset toils, experimenting on volunteers and animals with stem-cell gels and plasticine patches. They imagine future Acolytes with skin stretch behind them like sails or fashioned into elaborate woven garments.

"Where my misguided colleague fails," my Earthly Master would say of the freak Von Knopka, "is when he insists that the body is an anchor, something that restricts access to the outer realms. He thought that separating consciousness from the body could be obtained by physical subtraction, an elimination of mass that would allow the mind to float beyond upper echelons. But we understand the truth, that the body is an antenna! Not something to be cast aside, but built upon. Not something to be forsaken, something to transform."

It's difficult to convey just how important drugs are in our community: For pleasure, for exploration, and for ceremonies, yes, but also for our ultimate survival. The dangers of prolonged life underground include weak bones, colon cancer, Hodgkin's lymphoma, ovarian cancer, high blood pressure, pancreatic cancer, and prostate cancer, to name a few. A nutritionist proactively combats these potentials with a calculated diet and exotic supplements. Prolonged life underground can cause intense mental stress but our psychiatrists manage this with chemicals designed to promote empathy, stability, and love.

My Earthly Master's roots reach back to the original psychedelic revolution. In addition to Leary and Kesey, we study the works of William S. Burroughs, Carlos Castaneda, Aldous Huxley, and Hunter S. Thompson. As a cautionary contrast, we examined the failures of MK Ultra, Project Wormwood, Operation Midnight Climax, and the Ladder Study which used

BZ, or 3-quinuclidinyl benzilate, on US soldiers in Vietnam to maximize aggressiveness. We dissected the work of Terence McKenna. We believe that mushrooms and spores are actual extraterrestrials who traveled to this planet eons ago on meteorites. We advocate the theories of Dr. Rick Strassman, author of *The Spirit Molecule*. We believe DMT is a key to the ultimate doorway. And when we see the entities on the other side, they see us as well.

Yes, our drug use is copious and complex, constant and varied, as we continue to explore, as individuals and in groups, the outer limits of psychological expansion. Even those of us who were experienced with hallucinogens before becoming Acolytes find that drugs affect us differently after trepanning. Trips are more intense and can sometimes be unforgiving, especially doses administered through needles directly into the brain. Trips initiated in the right hemisphere hit different than trips initiated in the left hemisphere. And we have access to anything and everything in our compound, a depository that makes DJ's briefcase look like a kid's lunchbox. We use drugs individually at times, but most often in combinations. Taking a trip is like spinning a roulette wheel since one spin has no effect on the next. But all of us hope that, one day, one amazing Acolyte will receive the perfect combination at the perfect moment, the billion-dollar spin. The secret formula guarded by the Gods. And in that moment, all boundaries will break. In that moment, the entire Earth will tremble and satellites will fall from the sky. The lost Tribes of the Moon will be rattled from their slumber, inspired to return to the surface world to reclaim what had been stolen. And all of us lucky enough to witness the breakthrough will become Saints of the New Frontier(s).

I didn't know that I was psychic until after my trepanning. I've always had great gut-instincts, but nothing extraordinary. Everything changed after my heartbeat returned to my brain. It's as though I gained an invisible tentacle extending from my forehead, pulsating. It pulls knowledge from my surroundings like an animal drinking water, revealing hidden passages, delivering axioms, voices, and flashbacks. While blind to future events, I found myself able to understand aspects of strangers as easily as reading a book.

My Earthly Master is the exception. He remains mysterious to me.

I almost never had him to myself, like that time when he came to soothe me in the nothingness. He's ways flanked by followers and advisors, even lowly sycophants. He's almost never without his Alpha, an Acolyte named Selda. She is his most trusted confidant, his lieutenant, and his primary polyamorous lover. She's severe and cold. The only proof that she's alive is the beating of her heart, visible to everyone through the plexiglass window surgically installed over an area once occupied by her left breast, and through the ribcage.

Alone at last, we discussed my ongoing transformation, the manifestation of my true form.

"Sybil, you've heard the theory that losing one sense heightens another, haven't you?" my Earthly Master inquired.

"Of course I have." I replied.

"And you believe it's true?"

"Of course, Master Hauptnadel."

"Then," he said with a devious, satisfied smile, "give me your eyes."

Unlike the earthworm Von Knopka, Hauptnadel didn't want to eat my eyes. He only wanted me to retire them, put them into hibernation. And as he predicted, as science has proven, my other senses flourished once the Acolyte named October sewed my eyelids closed, senses I had been born with and senses awakened by my trepanning. It's ridiculous to believe that humans only have five senses. Without sight occupying a significant portion of my mind power, I developed north-sense, depth-sense, electro magnet-sense, spectrum-sense, and atmospheric pressure-sense. I could hear beetles burrowing a mile below me. The invisible tentacle extending from my forehead grew ten inches and bifurcated. Drug trips became epic, far beyond mere visual excursions into heavenly voids and vicious hellscapes.

But it wasn't enough.

The next time I found myself alone and in the presence of my Master, he spoke just a single word:

"Septum."

"Yes," I said. "I understand."

In anatomy, a septum is, quite simply, a wall. There are quite a few of them throughout the body. There are multiple septa in the heart, for example, and a septum on your tongue. There can even be a vaginal septum, although it's a medical anomaly and, frankly, not something I would wish on my worst enemy. The nasal septum, however, is unique within the body, not merely composed of cartridge, but bone. And it's bigger than you realize. The portions you often see pierced is but the columella, a comparatively soft strip of skin at the bottom. The nasal septum continues through the nose, all the way into the nasal cavities. It sits on the same plane that divides the brain into separate hemispheres, humans into left and right, reverse carbon copies of ourselves.

The removal of my septum represented a literal and figurative reconstruction. Dividing the brain's hemispheres will turn a person into a zombie, as any lobotomist will attest. But what if this wall no longer existed? What if the two halves became one? The creative and the analytical combined, allowing for billions of new neural pathways to form, previously impossible connection. The removal of my septum represents the unification of self, the merging of extremes, the polarization of opposites.

It was a bloody affair, presided over by my Earthly Master, performed by our top resident surgeon, attended by my entire tribe. We designed a procedure that would culminate with the surgical closure of my mouth, as I had seen in a vision. It wasn't done to subtract another sense, rather as a means of focusing my sensory receptors. The surgeon and I realized that, by removing a significant portion of my hard palate, my maxilla, I would be able to eat. Not normally, per se, but without debilitating complexity.

We began ritualistically. A hook on a chain descended for the rafters of the cathedral. I attached the hook to my septum ring and was hoisted aloft. As anyone with a septum ring can tell you, that columella is a tough fucking bastard. It took gravity a while to rip me from its clutches. I tumbled to the hard wooded floors of the cathedral, gushing blood. Gushing with emotion.

Before surgery, as is customary, my Earthly Master removed the plug in my forehead, the device designed to prevent bone spurs from forming along the borders of the portal. As supreme anesthesiologist, it was his duty and his pleasure to inject me.

"Nothing for the pain," I begged him. "I want this."

My Earthly Master smiled, considered the contents of his finger syringes, and plunged a needle into my brain. To allow my brain additional room to expand, he placed a glass globe over the opened hole. Colors burst. Blood and adrenaline surged. And I submitted to the most significant step in my transformation, my journey towards my true form.

The Boatman had, unknowingly, started the process before I had even arrived. The surgeon removed four more teeth, arranging them neatly on the sub altar beside me. After removing all the connective tissue between my upper lip and my nose, he took a tool resembling bolt cutters to extract about one-third of my upper jaw. The crunch was exquisite. He was able to cut out, not only the cartilage portion of my septum, but 80% of the bone itself. I savored every moment, tears streaming down my cheeks.

The immediate results looked hideous. My face below my

nose was sunken in, flapping. Staples and stitches poked out from the wreckage. Things were tidied up, somewhat, when my mouth was sewn shut, adding resistance to the fresh wound. The surgeon and I had collaborated on an apparatus to hold everything in place to set and heal. A surgical steel halo, the size of a large plate, held in place by hooks installed in the back of my skull. Wires extending from the halo at measured intervals pulled my mono-nostril taut into the shape of a triangle. The surgeon signaled the procedure's conclusion and unveiled me, dripping blood and mucus. All of the Acolytes applauded my ascension.

I would be attended too for quite some time, kept on a strict regimen of liquid nutrition and antibiotics. I was advised to sleep, although I was sorry to do so, as it separated me from the torturous bliss of healing. But like all wounded beasts who defy death, I healed. It wasn't long before I was out of my quarters, transformed and rejuvenated.

As expected, my abilities were further enhanced by my radical facial reconstruction. My hearing was exceptionally astute, able to pick up and process multiple conversations whispered simultaneously in the farthest corners of the compound. A new form of vision began to develop, a sort of echolocation that resonated in my expanded nasal cavities. The invisible tentacle emerging from my forehead grew and further divided, becoming a foursome of sub-tendrils, quivering like whips, pulling information from the atmosphere. The removal of my hard pallet gave my tongue access to the soft walls encasing my brain, as well as the optic nerves behind my eyes. I learned how adding pressure to specific areas produced euphoric affects, magical visuals.

I took to walking on all fours in order to align my brain horizontally with my heart. Rather than moving forward with a loping gait like a gorilla, I moved sideways with the speed and precision of a crab. I scurried along halls and corridors, through chambers and antechambers, through all the pews in the cathedral, having the time of my goddamn life.

How long had it been since I joined the Acolytes of Ascension? Impossible to calculate. Unlike the heretics and hypocrites who inhabit Terminal Island, we've abandoned any semblance of alignment with the Earth's rotation. We don't use clocks, nor do we eat or sleep on set schedules set within a twenty-four-hour parameter. It doesn't get light or dark in our compound. It hovers at just about dusk, illuminated primarily by candlelight. And, as such, we are no longer slaves to the artificial constraints of time. Day and night have become foreign, antiquated concepts. "Month" and "year" have become measures of intensity, divorced from the actual passage of time.

What else can I reveal to you about the Acolytes of Ascension? What other misconceptions can I correct?

Yes, we have sex. Voracious, sometimes indiscriminate sex. Rarely tender, often extreme, always consensual. We have sex for pleasure and stress release, but always attempt to make the practice a sacrament through the incorporation of rituals, specific stimulants, and apparatuses designed to enhance sensations. It isn't for the faint of heart or the timid or the proud. Solo or in tandem, in groups of every size, in jubilation, in reverence, and in sport. Power is exchanged and harnessed. Bonds are established and shattered and reborn. Depraved. Magic. Exquisite.

But there's a sadness underneath it all. A quiet desperation. Because our congregation understands that everything can end in an instant. Beyond the same cosmic dread that haunts every man and animal, we suspect an extinction level cataclysm is eminent. Our ultimate survival depends on the work we do here, our collective ability to adapt and evolve to unknown changes. Change is coming. We hear it bellowing up from the depths below us like starving giants locked in combat. We enjoy this harmonious existence while it lasts, optimistically nihilistic in regards to the coming storm.

Our time is occupied by trials and exercises. We spill blood, burn and scar our flesh, hang suspended by hooks over blistering hot coals. We imagine and invent new tools for suffering. We test new methods of infliction. Our time is occupied with music, dance, art, and vigorous debate. Our time is occupied preparing for the future, through psychic exploration and technological advancement. Though thoroughly dissociated from the surface, we aren't truly self-reliant. I don't know how the food staples arrive, where our clean water comes from nor the steady flow of drugs and alcohol. But I know they won't continue to arrive forever. One day, we will be set adrift to fend for ourselves.

There are fewer of us now than there used to be, so I am told, a fact that explains the sense of depletion that sometimes lingers in the alcoves like a foul odor. My Earthly Master and the older Acolytes regale us with stories from the pioneer days, a grander era when our halls were never empty or silent, when blood and semen stained every wall. Our dwindling membership is a source of both practical and philosophical concern. There are Acolytes who crave reproductive freedom, or at the very least, permission from my Earthly Master to breed. But there are "complexities" he assures us without explaining them, that make such propositions impossible, "at this time." My Earthly Master prescribes birth control to all Acolytes of reproductive age. Unplanned pregnancies are detected early and eliminated chemically. If our number are ever to swell again, recruitment will become essential.

But recruitment into the Acolytes of Ascension is rare and nebulous process. Most of the originals were nominated. Those they nominated identified the next group of cadets. The originals spent the 1990s and early 2000s selectively scouring renegade art shows, clandestine conventions, college campuses, and, yes, even Goth and S&M clubs in an effort to identify extraordinary potential members. All that changed in the Internet Era, when the congregation's existence was threatened with exposure.

Establishing residence underground, along with the need for secrecy, effectively ended the open recruitment era of The Acolytes of Ascension. It was both a necessity and a matter of practicality, as simply making the journey to the surface is a complicated ordeal, something I can personally attest to. In rare cases, however, exceptional candidates are identified. Acolytes have served as emissaries, returning to the surface for new blood.

Others find us through a combination of perseverance, luck, and happenstance. They find passage to Terminal Island where they make contact, inevitably getting wrapped in The Forlorn Order's red tape. Some pay exorbitant fees to runners, a loose confederate of guides and sympathizers offering transport to the Frontier(s) by circumventing all official channels. It's a dangerous prospect that comes with no guarantee of acceptance. Some attempt to find us completely on their own, beginning their journeys in the storm drains just below the Las Vegas Strip. They arrive tattered and cold like refugees, like humble peasants seeking sanctuary. I can say this because I was no different.

Except that I was different, wasn't I? I didn't decide to join The Acolytes of Ascension. I was identified by my Earthly Master after enduring a ritual in Pavia that created cosmic ripples. My pain was so extreme, so concentrated, so powerful it was detected, quantified, and communicated across thousands of miles, millions for all I know. And he heard me, my Earthly Master. And he collaborated with The Great Pendulum and His minions in order to reach me, to set me on my course, to deliver me. Yes, I had completed my cadet training the same as any other. I endured the indignities. And I did so happily, never deterred in the certainty that I would soon ascend. I am special, aren't I?

And it was this sense of pride, deserved or otherwise, that

added to the sting of his arrival: The lost soul. The fractured, spastic addict. The man who fell a mile through the firmament. He never asked to be an Acolyte, had never even heard of us, and seemed repulsed by everything about us—understandably so. And, at first, he seemed unlikely to live, never mind endure our ceremonial rituals. What made him attractive? He wasn't special. He wasn't even worthy.

But my Earthly Master is constantly looking for signs, and the outcast's arrival was interpreted as such. Unequivocally. He didn't believe in coincidences.

"This signifies the end of the beginning!" my Earthly Master exalted. "This man will receive my personal attention."

I would have left him outside to rot, let his festering meat attract the creatures in the darkness. Let them carry his bones away into oblivion. And of course I was right. Wasn't I? Because I'm a psychic. And they should have listened to me. And this was before I'd even examined him, smelled him, allowed my invisible tendrils to lap his face. His arrival signified the beginning of my end with The Acolytes of Ascension.

A bolt of blue lightning obliterated my surroundings and I found myself in the presence of The Great Pendulum for the first time since my transformation. I sought the equivalent of a warm embrace from an old friend, but received an odd chill. It took me a moment to notice that there was a wobble, to realize that The Great Pendulum had somehow been knocked off its axis.

A symphony played its final apocalyptic note into infinity.

Descent

Just because our past lives, our surface lives, become irrelevant to the committed Acolyte doesn't mean we stop thinking about them. There was a boyfriend I was fond of, quite some time ago. I met him at Sacramento's premiere bi-annual horror convention, Sinister Creature Con. His name is Caleb Peterson. He was the first person to tell me about the existence of McKamey Manor.

There's a subculture in the horror community dedicated to haunts, elaborate haunted houses that pop-up every fall in cities and small towns across America. Haunters are a fanatical breed, committed to creating fearful, gory memories to last a lifetime. It takes a team of artists, actors, engineers, and investors, most of whom spending an entire year preparing for the Halloween season. But McKamey Manor, located outside San Diego, isn't considered a haunt.

Russ McKamey, the proprietor of his namesake Manor, calls it "survival-horror bootcamp" but even that description falls short. Participants must sign a forty-page waiver, a document that lists possible risks including having teeth extracted, being tattooed, and having fingernails removed. "Tours", which run year-round, last between eight and ten hours, although no-one has ever made it all the way to the end. Even with the promise of a twenty-thousand dollars cash prize.

Of course I wanted to go. And even though there were twenty-thousand names on the wait-list, a last-minute cancelation gave Caleb and I the opportunity of a lifetime. It coincided with our two-month anniversary. We were "kidnapped", "tortured", caged, drenched, forced into freezers and coffins, made to put unknown substances in our mouths, induced to vomit, terrorized, nearly deafened, covered in tar, and summarily humiliated. It was the most romantic night of my life. And even though Caleb tapped-out around the three-hour mark, I persevered. I continued screaming and squirming, and gagging and weeping. And every time they asked me if I'd had enough, I'd reply, "Are you fucking kidding me?"

After thirteen hours, Russ begged me to call it quits so his crew could get some sleep. And though I could have endured for days, considering it child's play, he offered me five-thousand dollars to quit. He also wanted me to sign an NDA along with a statement claiming I had, indeed, tapped out before the scheduled end of the planned experience. I could hear him bitching as Caleb and I walked back to our car.

"Another fucking sadist."

When I set goals for myself, I become obsessed with achieving them. It was true when I lived under the Sun and it's just as true when I became an Acolyte of Ascension. My new goals included mastering telekinesis, making contact with the DMT elves, and acquiring the ability to see into the future. I wanted to reabsorb our most revered texts. I couldn't read them with my eyes, but my echolocation has become so precise, I could discern ink from paper. I wanted to explore the dangerous gorges and canyons that surrounded our lair, the violent and exhilarating promises of The Frontier(s). I wanted to manifest a bright future for my tribe, a testament to the voyagers who will follow us. All worthy goals, my Earthly Master assured me. And there was even more that I wanted to accomplish. And I would have accomplished them, all of my grandiose goals. But then he arrived, that motherfucker, and fucked-up everything.

The lost soul, the man who fell through a hole in the firmament, the addict first considered a divine providence, proved to be an utter disappointment. Good riddance! I was happy when he left and planned to think nothing more of him. Planned to turn my attention back to truly worthy endeavors. It would have pleased me to forget him entirely, erase those days when he diverted attention from my Earthly Master that could have been mine. And I would have.

How long had it been since the stinking liar's departure? Of course I can't say. But the unexpected visit from a representative of The Forlorn Order cast an unsettling gloom over our already bleak aesthetic. He spoke of signs from up above, of a potential infection, and of him, the wretched degenerate. They suspected he could be a catalyst, a bringer of calamity and rebalancing. Absurd! I rolled my eyes, even though they're sewn shut. I gave a dismissive scoff that sounded like a snort. The representatives wanted a complete accounting of his time in our compound, his words and activities, in excruciating detail. They insisted I make a personal statement.

Since my new voice was difficult for outsiders to comprehend, my Earthly Master decided to install a port directly into my brain, through my trepanning portal. This way, I could "dictate" my account mentally to AI-enhanced translation software used by the UN. I imagined we looked silly, me with a cord dangling from my brain, annoying my invisible forehead tentacles, plugged into my Earthly Master's laptop. How absurd was it that my Earthly Master even had a laptop! We laughed. A rare moment of levity between us.

He was never kind to me. Not like I imagined. Not like in my visions, even when I was certain it was really him, when he held me close and we were one within an astral chamber. He wasn't everything I dreamed. But he was worthy. Intelligent, engaging, inspired. As much as he honestly aspired to be godly, he was also pragmatic, realistic. He knew his age and feared the unknown. He's only human after all. And he was human in that mundane moment, in his lab, beneath the sick glow of his computer.

"Sybil, I'd like to touch your feet."

I didn't like people looking at my feet much less touching them, my soot-black, never-healing, oozing soles. But an Acolyte does what her Earthly Master commands. So I let him touch me, smell me.

"Extraordinary," he muttered. And he kissed me. He licked my feet. It was the most intimate moment of my life. We made a pact to never speak of it again, lest his Alpha, Selda, consider herself slighted by an errant whisper.

The representatives of The Forlorn Order left and returned with a list of follow-up questions. Then they left and returned a third and final time. They were accompanied by a permanent resident of New Bangkok, a controlling Sub-Architect of The Forlorn Order, a man of immense power and stature. So much so, and despite the ongoing territorial disputes that persisted between our two camps, my Earthly Master showed him an inordinate amount of respect, acted with an immensity of etiquette and decorum.

This time, the Sub-Architect requested, no, demanded a private audience with my Earthly Master. It didn't matter. I could have been a mile away and, with proper control, heard every word they said. And I should have run the instant they began talking about me, as every fiber of my being pleaded. Taken my chances in the chaotic chasms below. I might have if I had known what The Great Pendulum had in store for me. But who was I to abandon my Earthly Master, to deprive myself of my tribe, to throw away everything I had worked for and every obstacle I looked forward to conquering. But by the time they summoned me, my fate had already been sealed.

Who could have imagined that the Apocalypse would be such a political affair?

The Sub-Architect wore the head of a buck. Not a mask fashioned to look like a mighty deer head, the actual head. Of course it had been processed and customized to his physical dimensions. When he faced you, the buck's dead eyes bore deep into your soul. His ten points, filed into spikes, glistened. His actual face, this man's face, was behind the buck's neck. I could barely detect the camera that offered him vision within. The speaker he spoke through, however, the device that amplified and disguised his voice, was much more obvious. He was wearing a dashing suit that must of been at the height of fashion during Jack the Ripper's killing spree in Whitechapel.

He sat in our luxurious lodge room beside a raging fire. His chair was comfortable and elegant enough to have been a throne. He was flanked by several of his representatives, your stereotypical men in black, faithful administrators--including my former Underseer. My Earthly Master was there, of course, sitting on an elegant and intimidating chair that nonetheless looked childlike compared to the Sub-Architect's seat. He was flanked by his key Acolytes, including Selda, his Alpha, who stood by his side. Her heart seemed to be beating extraordinarily fast. All eyes fixed on me as I scuttled in on my hands and feet.

They had been making plans for me. There was no room for debate or counter-offers. My destiny had been dissected by committees, debated in subterranean parliaments, and commanded by a cabal of unimaginable capabilities. If I had died, they could have reached into the afterlife, had they desired, in order to snatch me back, to force me into completing their assignment. There would be little delay in setting me down this new path they had laid out before me. I can't tell you if it was day or night, but I knew for certain that it was my last hour with the Acolytes of Ascension. Everyone's insistence of the contrary brought me no comfort.

It's all his fault, that interloper, that fucking dickhead! Wherever he had gone when he left our compound, it had caused quite a stir, something that was continuing to reverberate throughout the columns of Hades. He had now officially been dubbed The Catalyst, a title as lofty as it was underserved, I was certain. He may or may not be carrying an infection. I was unable to penetrate the Sub-Architect's thoughts regarding this matter. The deer head, no doubt, prevented such intrusions. Whatever the case, he had been exposed to something extremely dangerous, something capable of denigrating the very fabric of our reality.

I sensed a collective, nebulous fear emanating from the Sub-Architect's representatives. It had to do with machines that were smaller than insects, smaller than germs, ravenous and capable of self-replication. They imagined all organic matter consumed, the planet left covered in a glistening layer of gray ectoplasm, an insidious, electrical jelly. They imagined black skies and red lightning, a collective-consciousness chanting a maddening, eldritch mantra. They suspected The Catalyst may have already set mechanisms into motion. Some were certain it was already too late.

Though he had spent a relatively short amount of time with us, my unique interaction with the dreg, the reject, the abysmal addict, had left indelible imprints. I'd be able smell him through rock and iron from five miles away. This made me the ideal candidate, the Sub-Architect explained, "for discerning his location and procuring his retrieval.

"It's not overdramatic to say:" Sub-Architect's buck eyes were searing with intensity, burning me, "everything in the world hangs in the balance."

To that end, I was to be transported immediately to the subterranean facility housing Tesseract Unit 23. No time for goodbyes. No going-away party for me. Still the insistence that, once my work has been completed, I'll be reunited with my Earthly Master and tribe. A pale prospect. An empty promise. Still, I was taken in a processional that had all the hope and fortitude of a mass funeral. It was a two-day voyage, including an eight-hour conveyance by private bullet train. While my secondary senses helped me place the facility in relation to the Acolytes' compound, I have no surface reference to give you. All I can say is, Tesseract Unit 23 is located at an immense depth. The facility housing Tesseract Unit 23 is a macabre, desolate garrison with all the warmth and vitality of an abandoned arctic research outpost. At its center, the device, an intimidating, almost ineffable machine.

Having read *A Wrinkle in Time* in grade school, I already knew what a tesseract was: A portal through space allowing for instantaneous transport between two locations. A wormhole, essentially. In more advanced literature and media, tesseracts are described as technological marvels, complicated feats of astrophysics. But a tesseract can also be created, harnessed, by a team of well-trained mediums and occultists. The machine known as Tesseract Unit 23 is somehow both and neither. Like an artifact of dead gods, reverse-engineered and refurbished, maintained by a small legion of devotees dressed entirely, exclusively, in white.

Astronauts train for years before a mission. Scuba divers spend months becoming certified. Even a skydiver must complete three tandem jumps with an instructor before they're allowed to jump solo. So how much training do you think I received, Sybil the Space-Jumper, before I was strapped into a tin can and blasted into oblivion? Barely three hours.

My head was shaved and all of my metal modifications were removed, for safety. I was pushed into a form-fitting latex suit. Then my torso, arms, and legs were coated in a waxy, translucent substance that smelled vaguely like lavender and plasma. Sensors, monitors, trackers, communication devices; I was covered in them. The team of devotees in white scurried around me like animated animals preparing Cinderella for the Ball.

Dr. Bram Bloodsaw was the chief scientist at the facility that houses Tesseract Unit 23. He gave me my final instructions as I was being strapped into the primary stargate module.

"You'll be making up to five jumps total" he explained. "We're sending you to coordinates associated with the Catalyst's last known whereabout. When you find him, activate your transponder beacon. We'll send troops to retrieve you from the nearest active barracks." Noises from the machinery powering on quickly built into a menacing groan. "If you don't activate your transponder beacon, you'll automatically jump to the next set of coordinates every sixty minutes."

Two days ago, I was living my wildest dreams as a devoted Acolyte of Ascension. Now, as other components of the capsule were assembled around me, I felt like Lika, the first animal launched into space as part of the Soviet space program. Lika died in orbit because they never planned on retrieving her. Maybe I had acquired the ability to see the future after all. I cried.

"Don't be scared," said Bloodsaw, mistaking my tears of sadness for fear. I thought about my Earthly Master, about how he hadn't even come to the doors of the cathedral to wish me goodbye when I left. As though he couldn't bear to look me in the eyes.

But he did care. How could I doubt it. Even then, as the countdown was initiated, I carried a piece of him with me, inside of me. Inside my vagina.

"Take this," my Earthly Master told me as we passed in the corridors for the last time. His voice was hushed to the point of being subliminal. He feared detection by the representatives.

"What is it?" I asked him.

"A lifeline, my child. If all else fails."

The facility housing Tesseract Unit 23 was functioning at maximum. Sounds of stress and strain merged into an ominous groan. Metal girders seemed on the verge of buckling, sparks erupting from terminals, sirens and sub sirens competing for attention. Devotees scrambling, pulling levers. The countdown nearing its final digits. A group of five surrounded me like the points of a pentagram, raising their arms to Heaven as if hoping to channel the powers of the gods.

"Sybil, can you hear me?" It was Dr. Bloodsaw, testing the audio connection in my earpiece. I indicated that I could with a middle finger. "Sybil," Dr. Bloodsaw continued, "What do you suspect is the key to tesseract travel?"

Of course I knew the answer, and we said it in unison:

"Pain."

I was hit with an intense wave of white light and Gamma radiation that was utterly unique yet somehow familiar. A new threshold. And with this new mile marker came an epiphany in regards to my participation in this operation. I had endured a level of agony in Pavia that was so unprecedented, it registered on a cosmic Richter Scale. My ability to suffer is mythical. And the reason mankind isn't already using tesseracts as military technology to rip each other to shreds is because no one alive can withstand the pain. No one but me. Ruptured Achilles tendons, Shingles, broken ribs, childbirth: These are the conditions considered most painful for a human to endure. I eat these sensations for breakfast. Spanish Boots, Catherine Wheels, Brazen Bulls, Iron Maidens—bring them on. You've got a Pear of Anguish? I'll crush it with my Kegels and throw it away like a tampon. Because I am the Queen of Pain and I alone can transverse these forbidden doorways, plumb these excruciating portals. I am legend.

Over a period of five jumps, one per hour, I visited five ungodly realms of horror. Each stop, a shocking wonderland I could have easily lost myself in forever. Each stop a life-altering, mind-shredding descent past madness and back again. Each stop worthy of a thousand-word tome, surpassing even the curiosities of lost Carcosa.

They sent me to Hell. A realm with an oppressive with a "Barker-esque" aesthetic. A Judeo-Christian nightmare intensified beyond extremity. A daunting labyrinth, a sinister maze, miles in height and unfathomable in width. Levels of stairwells and archways, corridors and sub-corridors, and sub-sub-corridors teaming with shadow-people, demi-demons, and hounds. Flayed bodies litter the landscape, stacked like cords of wood, creating ponds of blood. Behind locked, wooden doors came the sounds of suffering, human agony, pain and guilt and, of course, profound regret. Each room a Hell within a Hell. The sky above was roiling with storm clouds, spewing great red shards of lightning that fractured into faces of grim defiance. At the outer fringes, berserkers and titans crawled and clashed, feasting on carrion, lost in a state of perpetual amnesia. From all corners of the horizon, columns of the damned stream forward, machining in unison like soldier of the dead. I found an abandoned tower, climbed to the top and then out onto the crumbling, cylindrical rooftop. Impossible winged beasts encircled me, screeching and snapping. I sought the derelict, the fucking Catalyst, inhaling brimstone and rot, hot winds and blistering dust. He was nowhere. In Hell, every second is an hour, every minute is a year, every hour is a lifetime of crushing anguish. I did not leave this land unscathed.

They sent me to a garden of unearthly pleasures and unspeakable disorder, a realm both godly and ghastly. A collision of worlds, Hieronymus Bosch and H.R. Giger, William S. Burroughs and Junji Ito. The primitive, the alien, and the impossible. It can only be called a city, because no other word applies, but it was unlike any city made by man, occupying a cavern of superior enormity, illuminated by the orange and purple emissions of a volcano. The races that swarmed and squirmed over fields and neighborhoods only appeared to be human. Some were pale, some were black, and some were blue. Some were the size of lemurs and others were giants, towering above the spires and monuments. Heads and limbs were elongated. Chins, brows, and noses severely out of proportion. The creatures that had been domesticated were scaly and somehow aquatic, adorned with claws and fins and appendages that beckoned with hypnotic bioluminescence. The air was crowded with sound of drumbeats, riots, dissonant choirs defying maximum and minimum octaves, and organic machinery that churned with sinister, uncompromising purpose. I scurried and hopped through the metropolis like a jumping spider, like a supernatural ninja skulking unseen through the muddy street and across slippery rooftops. I pointed my mono-nostril into every corner of every sector, cataloging a million alien scents and sensations, but never detecting a whiff of the pathetic asshole, the troublesome Catalyst.

They sent me to The Backrooms, the pocket dimension cracked by A-Sync, a research and development corporation located in San Jose, California, back in 1989, an event that triggered the Loma Prieta earthquake. The Backrooms: Nine-hundred and ninety-nine-million square miles of liminal dread, a hellscape of damp, beige carpeting that reeks with mildew and maddening yellow wallpaper, sporadically illuminated by low-wattage bulbs in canned recesses, exasperated by impractically high and low ceilings, pointless columns, and perilous pitfalls. Originally explored as potential for storing nuclear military waste and undesirable portions of the population, The Backrooms ultimately proved impossible to pioneer. The architecture morphs and reassembles at random, or at the behest of an unknown intelligence. Some hypothesize The Backrooms itself is alive. Researchers encountered unknown toxic elements, biological hazards, and time anomalies. Worse, The Backrooms were never unoccupied as scientists at first insisted. There are beasts that roam these hallways, nebulous, bellowing fiends. Worse still, A-Sync has long lost control of the threshold that connects us to The Backrooms, leading to a spike in cross-dimensional "glitches", people disappearing, falling through cracks. While merely a nuisance now, this state of disrepair will eventually threaten the stability of both dimensions, ensuring cataclysmic repercussions. Even if the ugly Catalyst had become trapped here, I could have sought him out for a century without success. Nonetheless, I sprinted in an outward spiral beyond my control, dodging men in hazmat suits, panicked pedestrians, and bacterial monstrosities. Unbelievably, I spotted my old friend Byron from my old life, from my club and festival days. While I was excited to see him, he didn't recognize me. Unable to speak a common language, he turned and ran from me in terror. Damn The Backrooms. I couldn't wait for my time there to end, even though each jump had proven more painful, more taxing than the one that preceded it.

Traveling via tesseract doesn't just ravage the body, it destroys the mind. I was a wreck by my fourth jump. The pain and rapid shattering of previous thresholds had ceased to be joyful, rewarding, redeemable. I sensed internal decay, the subtly sweet scent of rot. I coughed, expelling blood and mucus from my mono-nostril. I wasn't certain at all that I'd survive my final jump. Which is why I considered staying where I had crashed next forever. It was a land of humongous fungus, endless hills of giant mushrooms, a blissful twinkling haven, a not-too-vast oasis amid underground islands of putrescence and mindless violence, far away from the wars already raging beyond control. Brilliant green giants roamed the canopy, lazily strolling between the acre-sized mushroom caps. Larger than hippos, smaller than whales, wrinkled like tardigrades, their mass should have sent them careening to the cavern floor. But they bound like ballerinas on dozens of tip-toes, aided by sticky tendrils that shot from their skin, attaching to the walls of the cavern like retractable spiderwebs, like cables and bungie cords. The sky was alive with singing insects and stealth mammals. A signpost in the distance pointed the way to St. Martin's Land. I could smell enough clean water and nutrition to spend all my remaining years here, in peace. A well-deserved retirement from pointless suffering, a blissful hermetic existence. I was tempted to strip naked, to peel off my cosmonaut gear, to smash my trackers and transponders, any blinking light that might have betrayed my position--and just disappear. Fuck the limp-dick Catalyst and Dr. Bloodsaw and the Forlorn Order. Fuck Larry and his mind games. Fuck Clancy and Valero back in Pavia. Fuck my Underseer, Dr. Oscar Von Knopka and his fourteen wives. Fuck everything and everyone who would violently take what I might have otherwise happily given.

I can't say why I didn't stay. It certainly wasn't out of a sense of duty for my mission. Out of loyalty to my Earthly Master, perhaps? The sliver of hope that I might one day be reunited with my tribe? Had I simply waited too long to decide, lost my hour in a beautiful, uncanny moment of healing contemplation.

My final jump was my hardest jump. Not just incrementally, but exponentially. I know now that The Sub-Architect never actually intended for me to live this long.

I regained consciousness in a complicated network of caves and mine-shafts. My ear piece, which had emitted nothing but static during my jumps, was playing a pre-recorded message on loop.

"On behalf for The Forlorn Order, we'd like to thank you for your service. Your contributions to the program have been invaluable. We own the future. Rest in peace, Soldier. On behalf of The Forlorn Order, we'd like to thank you for your service..."

There was nothing special about this realm. A spelunker's paradise, to be certain, but devoid of life or wonder. There was nothing special about me anymore, nothing profound about Sybil the Acolyte. Wasted and wrecked and wretched. All I could sense was darkness. My echo-sight, muffled and blurred. My secondary-senses, gone. Unable to discern my depth, direction, or the position of the moon, I was adrift. An unknown cosmonaut lost in space, beyond the reach of even The Great Pendulum. My strength fading, my soul exhausted, I reached down between my legs and extracted my lifeline: An antique metal syringe. I clicked a button and its sizable needle extended like a switchblade.

I wept at this proof of my Earthly Master's love. I imagined the concoction would trigger a cosmic beacon, transport through the astra plane into pleasant sanctum where I would await psychic extraction by my tribe, reunited. I ripped the plug from my forehead and plunged the needle deep into my brain, scoring a direct hit to the pineal gland. The initial explosion was indeed glorious, immaculate, beyond imagination. But it was more than just a mega-dose, it was a transmission and a confessional. And it was an overdose.

He appeared to me in a vision, my Earthly Master, delivering his own pre-recorded communication, like a message in a bottle washing up on my fractured psyche. He never intended for it to end up like this. He harbored genuine affections for me. He believed in my unprecedented potential. But he didn't have a choice. The Forlorn Order takes what it wants, what it thinks it needs. "But your sacrifice, my child, has not been in vain," he assured me. "In exchange for your service, The Acolytes of Ascension have been granted full independence and immunity from all future intrusions. Enjoy your final ascension, sweet Sybil."

Utterly betrayed, I thrashed and writhed, finding strength in these new thresholds of rage. Then came the pleasure, a secondary tidal wave of opioid oppression, a warm and inescapable oblivion. Then came the poison, like icicles in my heart, like toxic waste in my stomach. Hot foam flooded my esophagus, spewing from my mono-nostril like a violent geyser. I fell paralyzed, nearly unable to pull breath into my withering lungs. Everything slowed as my brain prepared to release its final load of DMT.

A crack of blue lightning, the familiar scent of afterburn and ozone. He had found me! The Great Pendulum! Somehow back on His axis, realigned, delivering a singular message as loud as a million horns blasting.

"Survive."

Another bolt of epic blue lightning and I was back, trapped like an ant, but possessed with determination. I felt the earth trembling, rocks cracking and crumbling, the crushing boom of explosives in the distance. I clawed at my eyes, searching for the tiny knots in the stitches but growing impatient. I pulled and tore and ripped, nearly removing my entire right eyelid in the process, but I had reclaimed my sight. And not for nothing.

A stream of rocks, sand and dust spilled onto my head as a powerful drill bit broke through, screaming in triumph before retracting. A light came through the bore hole. Then the sound of a dog barking. And then a voice.

"Are you down there? Can you hear me?"

"Yes!" I screamed, tried to scream, but my modified nose was never intended to convey a voice. I clawed and my face, my lips, snapping knots and seams until my jaw exploded open with a mighty, bloody yelp.

"Don't move! We're coming! But we have to be careful not to cause another cave it."

"Where am I?" I croaked.

"Death Valley. My name is Justin Moorhead. I'm with Mojave Search and Rescue!"

Coincident or cosmic design? I didn't care. I was saved!

Cave rescues can take days, but I was elated. Rehydrated and fortified with a peanut paste, all that was required of me now was patience. Justin Moorhead arrived with Dave Brewster and Janice Russ. I was so wasted they needed to strap me to a gurney in order to get me out. They maneuvered me painstakingly through the tunnels and shafts on ropes and cables. I felt like Frida Kahlo being carried in a bed through the streets of Mexico City. I don't ever remember smiling so much.

"What the fuck happened to her face?" Dave whispered to Justin and Janice when he thought I had slipped into unconsciousness.

"Must have been hit in the face by a big-ass falling rock," Justin guessed and Janice agreed.

Sure. Believe what you like, my sweet rescuers. Don't burden yourselves with my sordid past, my self-destructive activities. I'm just some neo-hippy who fell through the desert while on a drug trip. It happens all the time. And wouldn't it be nice if it was all a dream? I'd never fled to Vegas, never suffered pointless rites of passage in order to gain entrance into a gutter city of extravagant sleaze. Never subjected myself to the manipulations of a madman, or madmen, who appreciated my body for its ability to endure punishment, my mind for its ability to calmly process atrocities.

Wouldn't it be nice if I could parlay all this trauma into a fresh start? Reemerge in a new city under a new identity. My face, irreparably modified, could never be connected back to Larry and all of that messiness in Sacramento. I don't have any identifying tattoos. I've never donated my blood to an ancestry deciphering service. It's almost too perfect.

"But how will I explain my stitches," I wondered as my rescuers prepared to maneuver me past a final obstacle, revealing a pillar of sunlight gushing from a shaft above. But as I reached up to touch them, they were gone. My eyes had been deprived of light but were otherwise undamaged. No stray knots or strands around my lips either. Maybe... maybe...

I had to laugh as the ropes snapped and I fell, ricocheting against rock walls, plummeting back into the pits of despair. Von Knopka and Hauptnadel hadn't been a dream. My rescue from

Death Valley had been. I found myself lying atop of pile of bones, animal, human, and unknown. From all corners of the labyrinth, I heard creatures hissing, moving in. Not to devour me. Merely to bask in my suffering.

What's a woman to do in such a position? The only thing she can do. She sells her soul to a demon, of course. It happens more often than you think. Those in the throes of a prolonged demise are often courted by the most opportunistic denizens of the underworld, promised a second chance, carrying the mythic elixir that all who fear death crave like heroin. I entertained my solicitors, the vilest legislatures from regions deeper than Hell. I found myself seduced by The King in Yellow, whose conditions I considered both sinister and pragmatic.

The contract was signed.

A symphony held its final triumphant note into infinity.

The earth vomited me back up to the surface bloody, oozing, reborn.

Ascent

My boyfriend Caleb Peterson broke up with me after "the scene" I caused at McKamey Manor. I scared him when I cackled hysterically, fought back against the "scare actors", and demanded they give me more. And more. Everyone could tell that I had been masturbating when they pulled me from "the coffin".

"What's wrong with you?" he asked after hours of silence driving back to Sacramento. But only hours of silence followed. No use trying to explain when the whole thing was ultimately pointless. We just weren't compatible.

But I still think about him fondly, I've never stopped. I smile at the irony, that a guy obsessed with horror movies turned out to be the most stable, safe, "normal" relationship I'd ever had. He's the one who introduced me to *Martyrs*, the infamous pinnacle of New French Extremity, a film widely regarded as one of the most disturbing, most depraved, most difficult to endure—ever. Released 2008, *Martyrs* is written and directed by Pascal Laugier, who includes an advanced-apology to his viewers in the form of a prologue on the *Director's Cut*. For the love of God and Satan, do not watch the 2015 American remake. Americans are addicted to their pointless happy endings.

For the uninitiated and the squeamish, *Martyrs* is about a secret torture cult obsessed with the afterlife, and their most recent experiment, Anna (played with gut-wrenching sincerity by Morjana Alaoui). By subjecting Anna to a regime of isolation, degradation, and brutality, they hope to push her slowly to the brink of death, close enough to see what's on the other side. After being nearly completely flayed, she enters a state of "martyrdom", smiling in quiet serenity at what lies beyond. The cult is led by the austere, esoteric, turban-capped Mademoiselle (played to chilling perfection by Catherine Bégin), who rushes to Anna's side, anxious to receive a detailed account before the "Martyr" ascends. What she hears, destroys her. Literally. Days later, the cult is gathered at a secluded manor, eagerly anticipating Mademoiselle's report, the culmination of decades of spiritual research. Secluded in an upstairs bedroom, her assistant checks in, reminding Mademoiselle that guests are waiting.

"Can you imagine what she told me?" Mademoiselle asks her assistant regarding Anna's revelations.

"I couldn't possibly," the bespectacled assistant stammers.

"Keep doubting," Mademoiselle replies, producing a pistol, eating the barrel, and blowing her brains out.

"God damn!" I gasped at the film's conclusion. "This movie is fucked up. Especially that ending."

"Well yeah," Caleb replied, "But it's so much more than that." He had seen *Martyrs* dozens of times and had ruminated quite a lot about it. He was eager to share his perspective. I wasn't used to hearing people speak so passionately about films, especially horror movies. "What do you think the ending means?" he asked me.

"It means Mademoiselle didn't like what she heard and took the secrets of the afterlife to her grave."

"Maybe," Caleb conceded. "Or maybe it's much more profound than that."

"What do you mean?"

"This cult, they'd been looking for answers for decades. Certainly they were pragmatic and objective enough to prepare themselves for bad news. They must have at least considered the possibility that Hell awaits us, or worse—nothing. So why did she do it? Why did Mademoiselle kill herself?"

"I don't know, Caleb, but I can tell you can't wait to tell me."

"She did it to save them," Caleb proclaimed emphatically.

"From what?"

"Forbidden knowledge," Caleb whispered ominously. "Whatever Anna saw becomes irrelevant. The point is, when you know the answer to everything, life loses all meaning. Going through the motions becomes unnecessary. When you know the meaning of life, there's nothing left to do except die. That's why Mademoiselle didn't have the heart to tell her constituents. She was saving them from her fate. She was saving us all from the Apocalypse."

I think about it a lot now that I'm in recovery. Not *Martyrs*, per se, but the idea that knowing the meaning of life makes living impossible. It's soothing. Those fucking Doctors, they were all able to seduce me with promises of an ultimate answer, and some small role for me somewhere in the chaos. Now that I'm out, now that I have a second chance, I won't be so obsessed with knowing why. I'll be content simply to be.

I regained consciousness in a hospital. But I promise you, this isn't one of those "and it turned out she was crazy all along" or "she was in a coma the whole time" kind of stories. Nothing so contrived or simple. Because life isn't simple and neither am I. And though I am very much a different person than I was when I began these recollections, I'm still Sybil, a woman of my own making, searching for her light and her tribe. Much has happened since I last recounted. But first, my confessional.

Before the first Pandemic, at an annual horror convention in Dallas, Texas, I attempted to assassinate Clive Barker.

Jason Phillips, the proprietor and chief fabricator of Nightmares Unlimited makes the best *Hellraiser* paraphernalia on the planet. Not just static Lament Configurations, he had models that would actually twist and spin into the Star Configuration and the Doorway Configuration. He makes unique models as well, like a Lament Configuration baring the faces of the four original *Hellraiser* Cenobites plus Frank and Kristy Cotton. And he makes sculptures, Lament Configurations that appear to be bursting chains, each capped with a hook, each hook clutching a scrap of flesh, the entire array dripping scarlet. He conducted his entire business through Facebook, and I contracted him, grudgingly at first, to create some custom pieces.

"I'm not sure," was his initial reply. "What you're asking for is, you know, dangerous."

"It's for a movie I'm making," I explained, "a *Hellraiser* fan film, obviously. I promise, we'll take all necessary precautions."

"I'm still not sure," he hemmed. "I could be held liable if..."

"Name your price." I still had plenty of my McKamey Manor money.

I knew that I'd never be able to fly with the devices he had fabricated for me, so I shipped them to a Fed-Ex drop off center located within the Dallas/Fort Worth Airport where I picked them up upon arrival. I checked into my room at The Marriott, the same hotel hosting the convention, and prepared for a moment I'd been imagining for years.

We've all heard the rumors, all hardcore Clive Barker fans. We've heard whispers that his epic visions truly represent a hellish netherworld, that he was given a peek at what lies beyond after signing a contract. Cursed to carry twisted visions, a soldier on a mission, spreading the gospel of grotesquery. But I'd become concerned. Concerned by internet chatter claiming he was in a downward spiral. That he had built himself a mansion of cocaine in Beverley Hills, but after decades of chasing demons, the walls were beginning to crumble in on him. Concern became obsession and obsession, I admit, became delusion.

Clive Barker was one of hundreds of featured guests at the convention and I was one of many thousands of attendees. Shoulder to shoulder with throngs of rabid horror fans, it was difficult to maneuver among the vendors and exhibitions. Dozens of Jasons, hundreds or Michaels, a thousand Art the Clowns plus screen-accurate manifestations from every indie and major studio franchise ever made. I too, was in "cosplay", for the very first time, in fact. Though, in my mind, I was somehow more authentic. Because I wasn't merely a fan here to collect memorabilia and some autographs. I was a woman driven, focused, burning.

"Can I take a selfie with you?" asked an enthusiastic hipster in a Suspiria t-shirt.

"Fuck off!" I replied, sounding like I had a bit in my mouth.

It took me an hour just to find Clive Barker's table, and I spent another ninety minutes in the line, waiting. My heart began racing. My palms moistened. Blood dripped from the corners of my mouth, and from my cheeks. I became impatient, watching all of the posers gushing over him, crying as he signed original pieces of art and first edition copies of *The Hellbound Heart*. Pathetic, embarrassing displays of emotion from insufferable sycophants. I remembered to breathe. "Focus," I whispered to myself, steeling myself for what was to come. "Any minute. Any moment."

And then it was me at the front of the line, me ushered forward for my ninety seconds with the legend, the myth, the master. Clive Barker. He was seated of course, but not in a conventional chair. He was in a wheelchair. He was hunched to the left side, almost unnaturally so. My heart ached, ached for his lost youth, his dwindling potential. Still, I stepped forward. And I smiled. And I gushed. Blood ran down my bottom lip, off my chin, and pooled in my cleavage.

Clive Barker tipped his sunglasses down in order to behold me in all of my glory: The ultimate Female Cenobite. Head shaved to shining, skin powdered and marbled. My dress, a black leather terror. My belt, jangling with the tools of my trade: Blades for slicing and cutting and gutting.

"Well, my Dear," Clive Barker beamed. "Don't you just look amazing!"

I smiled and bowed my head, "Thank you," I said, as gracefully as possible with an appliance piercing my cheeks, gravity pulling it like a lap-bar across my tongue, now turning a deep shade of purple. A thick gaged strip of industrial wire, meticulously crafted into a circle, wires connected to fishhooks superficially piercing my thorax.

Clive recoiled slightly at a fresh dribble of blood and the sight of my crimson teeth. "Very realistic," he marveled.

In my hands, a Lament Configuration, my gift to him, straight from the basement workshop of Nightmares Unlimited. I ordered, commanded my body not to tremble. Clive Barker hesitantly took it from my hands. He picked a side and held a black sharpie over the box's gold and mahogany surface, centimeters away from its hidden trigger.

"Who should I make this out to?" Clive Barker inquired

"Female," I replied, smiling, on the verge of triumph.

Clive Barker pressed his pen into the center dial, which spun rapidly before retreating inside, leaving only a hole.

"What the..."

His words were halted by a controlled burst from a hidden nitrous oxide canister. Even as the startled author dropped my offering, three chains, each caped with a barb hook, shot upwards hitting him square in the face. A direct hit!

"What the Hell!" Clive Barker screamed. His assistant, the man handling his money and headshots screamed. People in line behind me began to scream. Panic began rippling through the convention center.

One of the hooks might have pierced Clive Barker directly in the eye if it weren't for the sunglasses he arrogantly wore indoors. It cracked the glass lens. The second hook bounced harmlessly off his nose. The third had somehow taken hold on his left lapel. When Clive Barker jumped up, the box followed him, hanging down below his crotch. He held his arms out and yelled at his assistant, "Get this thing off of me!"

A security guard spotted me in the commotion, spoke into his walkie talkie, and began moving towards me. He was hampered by the crowd retreating from my epicenter, but he'd reach me in a minute. It was time to pull out the major artillery.

"I've come to take you home!" I exclaimed with all the glory of a defending angel.

As I pointed my hands, palms up, towards Clive Barker, chains were ejected out from contraptions attached to my wrists beneath the sleeves of my dress. These chains were bigger than the ones that had emerged from the first box, heavy and substantial. Each one was, of course, capped with a glistening barbed hook, hungry for flesh. They both hit Clive in the chest before bouncing harmlessly to the ground. I pressed the reset button on my left wrist, but the mechanism jammed. I pressed the reset button on my right wrist and the chain began to retract before the hook stuck in Clive Barkers table, upending it, sending the headshots and sharpies and cashbox flying.

By this time, people were screaming about someone with a weapon. Crowds pushed away. A stampede seemed eminent. Clive Barker was carried away by his assistant and a team of convention volunteers who certainly weren't getting paid enough to deal with this situation. The security guard finally put hands on me. In an instant, I was on the ground, beneath his weight. Defused and confused. Deeply disappointed yet somehow, proud of what I had accomplished. My bravery. My fortitude.

I was never able to explain to the court appointed psychiatrists why I did it, not in a way that made any sense to them. How could I tell them that I honestly expected the worlds of fiction and reality to collide? That I expected darkness to creep through the convention, mist to rise from the floor, dark hallways to appear in walls where hallways weren't before? That I expected the tolling of bells, the bellows of the Engineer, and the emergence of interdimensional travelers? That I considered my action righteous and necessary for the reunification of a wayward master and his original muses? Even at my most delusional, I knew it was best to suffer my disgrace in silence.

I'd like to take this moment to officially apologize to Clive Barker for any suffering I might have caused him. And I'd like to thank him, profusely, for declining to press charges against me. I'm also eternally grateful that the talented Mr. Barker has declined to peruse litigation against me in civil court. I was happy to sign his no contact order and do not plan on violating its terms now or ever. I'd also like to thank the Texas Department of Corrections for their fair and humane treatment, and the Honorable Judge Nancy Sanchez for her leniency.

Of course, it all seems so trivial now, the tragedy and drama of obsession and horror conventions. So insignificant when compared to what I witness during my four-hundred and forty-four days underground. I did the math: four-hundred and forty-four days from the time I boarded my Elevator to Hell until I was found outside the Las Vegas Rescue Mission, a homeless shelter, on West Bonanza Road. I was semi-conscious, stuffed into a filthy sleeping bag, my face, wrapped in bloody bandages. The poor volunteer who unwrapped me to assess the damage couldn't stop screaming, even after she was removed from the building.

My eyes were bleeding. My mouth was bleeding. The tip of my nose was black with rot, crusty like a giant scab, hanging precariously like a mound of ash at the end of a cigar. I remember a swirl of police, paramedics, doctors, and investigators.

Memories of my days at Summerlin Hospital on North Town Center Drive are staccato. Not fluid like film, rather static and piecemeal, like a scrapbook. More doctors and nurses and investigators. Surgeries and procedures, drugs at tubes, blood and tears. For a long time, I couldn't speak. Even after healing, my face was a mess. I refused to look at myself. They couldn't figure out who I was. They sent in a police sketch artist to create an image of what I might have looked like before the physical trauma. It didn't look anything like me. They assumed I'd been kidnapped, beaten, mutilated, and forced into sexual slavery. They didn't know where to send me. I was so low, stuck in such a pit, that I didn't fucking care.

My case had been referred to Dr. Elijah Lucas, a pioneering plastic surgeon with a focus in facial reconstruction following animal attacks. He's an absolutely beautiful human being. While I clearly had issues beyond my recent physical impairments, which I regarded as mere issues of vanity, fixing my face was a necessary step in my ongoing recovery. It had been relatively easy for Dr. Lucas to repair my eyelids and lips. Even my nose was salvaged using somewhat conventional methods. It was my septum and pallet, obviously, that proved most challenging.

Luckily, they were able to harvest enough bone from my hips to recreate a pallet. It was covered with mucus membrane created in a lab. A stem-cell serum promoted the regeneration of gum tissue. The roof of the mouth is surprisingly resilient. My missing teeth were replaced with high quality porcelain implants. After the bones set, they were able to essentially reattach the portion of my face that was stretched and excavated. My new septum is an engineered bio-polymer. With follow-ups and fine-tuning, it took weeks to complete and weeks more to heal.

I was transferred to Beacon in the Dessert Recovery Center near Crystal Springs, off Highway 93 for my ongoing convalescence. Here I remain.

Beacon in the Dessert is, as its name implies, in the dessert north of Las Vegas. Very secluded. It's a small recovery/rehabilitation facility that prides itself on giving their patients focused, customized treatment. They work with victims of extreme trauma as well as those who meet the definition of criminally insane. They also take privacy very seriously. While there are at least half a dozen other patients in this facility, I've never seen them. Only voices.

My Savior, Dr. Lucas is on the board of trustees for Beacon in the Desert, and he's the one who both facilitated my transfer and procured funding for my treatment. He's renewed my faith in Doctors in general. He's an angel on Earth, and I can't wait to meet him in person. Even though he's had his fingers inside my skull on numerous occasions, we've never officially met. I can't wait to thank him for everything. I've been assured he'll be stopping in to check on my progress just as soon as his schedule allows.

My secondary Savior, figuratively standing side to side with Dr. Lucas, is Dr. Francis Fournier, my trusted, dedicated psychiatrist. She's the first female psychiatrist I've ever had and I had no idea what a difference it would make. I'm sure male psychiatrists can serve most female patients extremely adequately. But it never worked for me before. There were two perceived barriers to communication. Too much taboo to attempt to explain. But I've had breakthroughs with Dr. Fournier, screaming, convulsing, ugly-cry breakthroughs!

It's because of her I can admit without shame that I like

pain. And it's not because I'm broken or crazy. Daddy didn't beat me up. I like pain. What must be so obvious to you, privy to my most private recollections, was so often impossible to express to the people closest to me. I like pain. And it was easiest to get my comfort from strangers, from people who wouldn't have to look me in the eyes afterwards. Because people can't accept that a pure female masochist exists. The very idea is synonymous with damage. Which makes the pure female masochists one of the loneliest souls on the planet, prone to falling into the clutches of mad scientists and sociopaths. But I like pain, and it's not because of dysphasia or neurochemistry or brain tumors. I've had CAT scans.

I like pain. I am the embodiment of the pure female masochist. But that's not all I am. I like pleasure as much as I like pain. I always have. And not as a remedy for pain. I enjoy both extremes deeply, but independently, like polyamorous lovers. Eros and Thanatos intertwined. And neither end of the spectrum define me, just like my sexuality doesn't define me. Just like the fact that I was once considered a talented photographer doesn't define me. Just like my criminal record doesn't define me. Every slave will be a master, every Jekyll has his Hyde.

I'm also a follower, and there's no shame in that either. Everyone is encouraged to be a leader, but we can't all be leaders, can we? And I'm not a follower in the blind sense, like sheeple being herded towards slaughter. When I find a leader I can truly believe in, I'm a powerful follower. A lieutenant, a beta-wolf, a task master, an enforcer. Being a follower doesn't automatically make me weak. Being a devoted follower makes me an absolute treasure. But it also makes me vulnerable to abuse, as my journeys have revealed. So who will I follow next, and will they be worthy? These are some of the things I think about now.

And when the bandages finally came off, when I'd finally mustered the courage to look in the mirror, I saw someone new. Not Darcy. Still mostly Sybil. But also a woman I didn't recognize. A woman transformed, and I don't mean by blade or ritual. I saw a woman transformed by suffering, but also by knowledge. I was so pleased to meet her.

Of course I haven't told Dr. Fournier specific details, because I can't. The Forlorn Order has spies everywhere, but more than that, she simply wouldn't understand. Most people simply aren't equipped to fathom the enormity of what's happening beneath the city of Las Vegas. It's too big for me to explain, too beyond my own comprehension of engineering and geological sciences. It would be counterproductive to even bring these topics up with anyone on the surface. Anyone, unless they'd actually been there. And if they had, ironically, they'd probably be just as likely to keep their mouths shut. And because it's terrifying! I don't enjoy lying awake at night thinking about signs and the Apocalypse. These are unpleasant thoughts that hamper my progression, mentally and physically. When it comes to the "injuries" I sustained in Las Vegas, who held me "captive", and where exactly was I, I just tell Dr. Fournier, "I can't remember."

But I don't think I'll ever "move on", not completely. In my alone time, when I meditate, I try to apply lessons learned with Dr. Fournier to some of the experiences I had underground. It's amazing how just a slight shift in perspective can lead to incredible insights. Even when it comes to words, seemingly objective, inflexible words. Even words with singular definitions can have vastly different interpretations depending on tone and context.

Like when I was in bed with Dr. Von Knopka and his wives, for example. That one who spoke to me, the one with the voice like a kitten or a baby, she said, "Never more in love." It had clearly been part of a collective effort to seduce me, to bring me into their folds. Or was it? Maybe she said, "Nevermore in love." Maybe she was trying to warn me, to communicate that their attempts at multi-consciousness had failed. That she no longer endorsed her husband's practices and theories, that she no longer even loved him.

Or even the first and only time The Great Pendulum "spoke" to me directly: "Hauptnadel!" I assumed but also felt in my heart that he was to be my guiding light, my "Earthly Master". The Great Pendulum led me to him, practically step-by-painful-step. But why would a deity do the bidding of a charlatan anyway? Why align with my "Earthly Master" at all? Had Hauptnadel forced The Great Pendulum's participation through the use of chemicals and incantations somehow? But then I wondered: What if the point wasn't for me to join the Acolytes of Ascension? What if I was supposed to lead them? What if I was supposed to be the new Hauptnadel, as foretold perhaps, as prophesied, and as commanded by The Great Pendulum? And what if this was what inspired my treacherous "Earthly Master" to betray me, to cast me out, to leave me to mummify in some dry corner of the Earth's crust? These are thoughts I consider now, in my meditations. I also ask myself, "What comes next?" and, "Where do I go from here?"

As for The Great Pendulum, I still believe He's a deity by definition, but something less grand, perhaps, than I gave credit for. The living manifestation of a sigil, perhaps, or an emissary for hire, maybe? A being able to convey paths and destinies. Ultimately, it doesn't matter. I've been leaning much more agnostic these days, in spite of everything I've seen. Convenient for a woman who signed a contract with a pre-pagan demon. But wherever I finally land, I'll always appreciate The Great Pendulum as a symbol, for its perfect symmetry, for its insistence on cosmic absolutes. In fantasy, I had always imagined myself riding The Great Pendulum on its weight, holding a bolt of light, ready to dive off at its lightest or darkest apex, twisting and writhing into infinity. It turns out I wasn't a rider. I was the tether, pulled between the extremes, with only one way to extend beyond my physical confines: To break.

I'm sure you're wondering about Larry and whether or not I plan on ever coming clean.

I already have. I had to face what I had done, especially after everything Dr. Lucas and Dr. Fournier did for me. They asked me about my identity, about my family, about who to contact. I couldn't lie to them, involve them in a conspiracy, use them to initiate my life as a fugitive. And besides, I wanted to confess. I was tired of the weight of it, the guilt of it.

The thing is, the more I tried to recollect exactly what happened on that night I stabbed Larry, the more uncertain I became about it all. What had once seemed so clear, set in stone, was now a bizarre hodgepodge of conflicting scenarios and glitched images. Almost like my memories had been corrupted. It's strange, because I'm certain I lived underground for over a year and I'm certain I survived tesseract transportation, remembering every detail of all of it. But I can no longer say with certainty what happened the night I stabbed a man back in Sacramento.

Dr. Fournier says this is normal, that the mind shields us from what it's not ready to process. "What's obvious," she explained, "is that there was a conflict that night, and he was the aggressor."

Still, by the time representatives from the Sacramento Police Department came out to take my statement, I was even more uncertain about what transpired. All I knew for sure is that I stabbed Larry, and I admitted as much. Case closed, right?

It turns out that, earlier in the investigation, police had uncovered a trove to illegal pornography on Larry's laptop. Now, nobody seemed excited by the prospect of opening a cold case of vigilante justice against a pedophile. Especially when the alleged perpetrator is the survivor of a kidnapping, torture, abuse, and most likely slavery—even if she has a checkered past. The Police Officers took my statement, then told me they'd be in touch. I didn't have to be psychic to know, by the tone of their voices, that this was the end of the matter. I still have to deal with the suppressed trauma and my personal guilt, of course. But legally, I think I'm off the hook for murder. It was incredibly fortunate for me, to be unencumbered as I'm about to be given this chance at a new lease on life, this rebirth. Almost too convenient.

But I'd be a fool to second-guess these and other blessings.

Dr. Ernesto De León is a dermatologist who specializes in tattoo removal. He donates his time to prisons, recovery centers, and battered women's shelters, removing gang or trafficking related identifiers, as well as anything that carries significant psychological baggage. This living saint has been visiting Beacon once a week since before I arrived. He's made dozens of passes across the soles of my feet with his electric wand. It was challenging work, but black tattoo ink actually breaks up easier under lasers than other colors. The key was exercise between session to increase my circulation, allowing my lymph nodes to expel the Italian ink. The pain, while nowhere near as intense as when I received the ink, was nonetheless exquisite. Now, when I look at the bottoms of my feet: Pristine! And still tough as leather.

And finally, I'm pregnant! The fact that I was able to conceive at all during my "Earthly Master's" draconian regime is almost miraculous. The fact that the embryo survived five tesseract jumps is scientifically inconceivable. Yet there he was, in my womb, so small they didn't even know that he was there until after my series of surgeries. If he's a boy, I plan on naming him Clive, of course. I'm due in about twenty-five more weeks.

They still call me Sybil, because, for the most part, I'm still Sybil. A woman of her own creation. But I'm quite a different person than I was when we first met, back at the start of all this, when I was so pissed off and indignant. So needlessly confrontational. I apologize if I didn't make the best first impression. And I wish you luck, as well, in your own personal descents and ascents.

Today is a special day. Dr. Lucas is coming to visit. Now that I'm healed and healthy, I can't wait to see him and to thank him. I owe everything to him; his generosity and his kindness have been beyond scope. Oh here he comes right now, along with Dr. Fournier, My Saviors. They're beaming at me and looking at one another with pride. I'm in my bed, bursting with love, allowing myself to cry.

Dr. Lucas is a tall and handsome man with long white hair pulled back into a ponytail. But I don't think he's trying to look "hip" or "rock 'n roll". I think he's too busy working medical miracles to bother with something as trivial and vain as a haircut. His face is a comfort to look at. He greets me, calls me "lovely", tells me I look amazing. And then comes to sit on the side of the bed. His voice is like a soft blanket, somehow familiar. I'm emotional mush.

Now he's leaning in with an air of profundity, choosing his words carefully.

Dr. Lucas asks, "Sybil, what would you say if I told you I could change your life forever by asking you five questions?"

A tragic symphony strikes its final heartbreaking note into infinity. The operatic equivalent of all the souls of Earth scream, seven Angeles and five Horsemen bringing Hell from above. Trumpets blast, twisting upwards into infernal octaves as Dr. Lucas grins. He has so many teeth. Too many teeth.

Sybil isn't here anymore. She is and she isn't. Split. Her physical form lies stricken with convulsions. Her consciousness, frantic and aghast, is attempting escape onto an astral plane, floating through the ceiling and above the rooftop, into the fading light.

Flashback. Dr. Lucas's voice. That night in Sacramento that changed everything.

"I won't sign the fucking contract!" Sybil screamed.

The voice on the phone laughed. It laughed and laughed the

most hideous laughter she'd ever heard. "In that case, we'll be seeing you soon."

"You'll see me in Hell," Sybil replied.

Back in the incinerating moment of repulsive revelations, Dr. Lucas and Dr. Fournier have called for a nurse. Sybil's body begins to heave as they proceed to intubate.

Outside, her consciousness finds itself inextricably anchored to its mortal coil. It's because of the fetus. It won't allow her to leave. She's unable to transition into a state of pure consciousness because of this needy ball of cells. It keeps her tied like a balloon, leashed. No further ascension.

"They must have found me when the port was inserted, when he plugged me in..." The thought occurs. Not in a brain or disembodied psyche, but somewhere, in the ether, before it fades into oblivion.

Sybil, floating, does her best to disassociate, tries to enjoy the desert sunset, the blues, purples, and pinks. But her attention is drawn to a flagpole near the entrance of Beacon House. It bears the Conjoined-Twins insignia. Her screams are now reverberating throughout the dome and all across the artificial sky.

Epilogue

"I'm a detective."

I love saying that. And it's true. I'm a detective because I detect. Just because most detectives are police officers doesn't mean you have to be a cop to be official. You don't need a badge to detect, to research and collect evidence leading to the resolution of mysteries.

"I'm a detective."

It just sounds so fucking Noir. Like, you can hear a raunchy saxophone wailing in a steaming alleyway somewhere. And in a city like Las Vegas, it feels timeless. No, I'm not an affiliated detective or a "licensed" private investigator. So what? It would probably be just as accurate to call myself a bounty hunter, and I'm not "licensed" for that either. Besides, it's all just a side-hustle. Just a way to keep that cash flowing. And the last thing I really want is for any of my associates to know what I'm doing. It wouldn't go over well in the crowds I run with, if you catch my drift. People come to Vegas in order to disappear, not to be found.

"I'm a detective."

I immediately know everything I need to know about a

person by how they react to that sentence. Those who have nothing to hide have nothing to hide, but those who have secrets reveal themselves in a thousand ways—and they don't even realize it. That's what makes me such a good detective. And that's what made Sybil so fascinating.

"I'm a detective."

She didn't fucking blink. Sybil, aka Darcy Rowan Evensen, didn't reveal a fucking thing. I'd never seen anything like it.

I first noticed her at The Whole-Year Inn, where I stay from time to time, a weekend here and a weekend there. I had a ground floor corner unit the day she moved in upstairs. She looked like a fucking zombie. I had her pegged for a junkie and a sex worker, and I say that without a shred of judgement. Just experience. But there was something unique about her. Everyone at "The Hole" is off in some way, marginalized. Myself included. That's just the type this place attracts. But there was something about Sybil. She was desperate, but also controlled and powerful.

I started to see her with bandages on her hands. Eventually, she kept her hands completely covered in plastic Walgreens bags. She'd cinch them around her wrists with medical tape or electrical tape and even duct tape. People do strange things to hide injuries or because of obsessive compulsions, but in Sybil's case, it seemed like neither. And both. I realized that she didn't belong there, in "The Hole" with the rest of us derelicts. She wasn't here to pass the time or simply disappear. She was on a mission. I could see it in the way she composed herself, the way she walked.

I could also tell that she was on the run. It wasn't because she was nervous or paranoid. No, Sybil had poise. But I knew she was on the run because I could smell it a mile away and my nose was wide open. And it didn't take long to match a name to a face. Like I said, I'm an excellent detective. And it wasn't that hard. A few hours at the library cross-referencing public databases against social media accounts and Reddit threads.

Sybil is Darcy Rowan Evensen, a suspect in the stabbing death of Larry Andrysiak in Sacramento, CA, I was sure of it. I was 90% sure of it. But I needed to be 100% certain before making a call on someone. That's part of my credo. That's why I decided to take a chance, knowing it could blow my shot at collecting a reward. That's why I decided to talk to her.

"I'm a detective."

Nothing. No fear or stress, or even relief. You'd be surprised how many people are relieved to be caught because they're so sick of running. Sybil was at ease and in her own world, calmly playing video poker, sipping a Seabreeze. Her left hand was shoved into a box. Yes, that was strange too. But I was just stunned by her poise. Here I was, sitting across from a fugitive having just admitted to her that I'm a detective, and this lady didn't give a damn!

Now if she hadn't acknowledged me at all, ignored me, that would have been a dead giveaway. Believe me, people try it. Like, reality isn't about to clobber them over the head as long as they don't acknowledge it. Like staring down a train when you should be dodging it. Sybil was too smart for that. Too smart and too brilliant. She practically egged me on!

For the sake of complete professionalism and transparency, even though I'm neither, I'll admit that I found Sybil extremely attractive. I found her septum ring to be... extremely sexy. I know, a detective smitten by a pretty dame. It's so fucking cliché. And it wasn't just physically. She was charming. She was confidant. She was radiating a strange, almost cosmic energy. And she let me prattle on about some of my extracurricular interests, which I found irresistibly redeeming.

But there was something wrong too. There was pain. Her eyes and voice and stamina might have been able to deny it. But she was sick. She had been fading over the weeks since taking up residence in "The Hole". She hadn't slowed down, mind you, but she was thinner. More than that, it was almost like she was becoming see-through.

Even after a good while chatting, I still wasn't certain that Sybil was Darcy. I mean, of course she was, but maybe I still had doubts. Or maybe I really wanted to have doubts. Either way, I was about to say goodbye for now, retreat to plan the next phase of my strategy when I spotted it in her—something kindred. She was an explorer, just like I am. I knew it in an instant.

That's my real profession: Explorer. It's what I've devoted my entire life to. Believe it or not, it's what brought me to Las Vegas. I know what you're thinking, that Las Vegas isn't a place for exploration in a traditional sense. But there's more going on beneath the streets of Las Vegas than you can possibly fathom.

See, ever since I was a little kid, I've been obsessed with the idea of life underground. I would dream about it. And when I got older, I learned so much about the past and the future. And the deeper I looked, the more I studied, the more I became certain that was something epic, something almost unbelievable literally right below our feet. Not just a world, but worlds. And not just natural wonders, but marvels of engineering that will blow your mind. Marvels that were not crafted by human hands. Now before you accuse me of wearing a tinfoil hat, let me assure you, I am not talking about aliens. Fucking aliens.

People report huge, silent aircrafts soaring across Arizona, emanating from mountaintops and disappearing into caves.

"Must be aliens," they say.

People report seeing E.T.'s that can breathe our air and speak our languages. They always have one head with two eyes and a mouth. They always have a torso, two arms and two legs, just like most animals who roam the earth.

"Must be from another planet," they insist.

The best UFO evidence in existence: Navy Pilots engaged with an object west of Catalina Island off the coast of California.

Described as a giant Tic-Tac, it first appeared on radar over the ocean, left vapor trails over the water, and then disappeared into the murky depths.

"Aliens!"

Are you fucking kidding me?! The mental gymnastics people are willing to do in order to convince themselves there couldn't possibly be a smarter species than man that's already here, sharing our planet—just as they have for eons. And not just in our oceans, but under our feet. Races that have existed for millions of years. Races of being that are smarter than us, stronger than us, and undoubtedly more unified than us. And they hold the upper hand, not just because of superior cultural ethics and technology. It's because we simply refuse to acknowledge what our ancestors considered common knowledge: There's life underground.

Easier to imagine godlike aliens from another galaxy.

But not everyone is fooled. And not everyone is blind. Plenty of people know the real truth. But they use their knowledge as power. They build barriers to separate us from the real truth. Those with the resources are already dividing up a new frontier, laying the groundwork for new cities and new societies, worlds within the world where they hope to start anew, after the fall. But even they represent just the topmost layer of a reverse ecosystem. And they want to prevent anyone from going beyond their established domain. Because they know that the deeper you go, the higher you get. Those are the realms I've been preparing to explore.

Obviously, I've gone off on a tangent. No, this isn't representative of my actual conversation with Sybil. We kept it relatively light. Still, I felt that she was not only a like-mind, someone open to the revelations I've uncovered, but a potential collaborator. I imagined us, together, finding extraordinary lost realms. Because, in her own way, she was already trying to find them.

She'd already heard of Elevators to Hell. They're practically an urban legend. But she seemed to have something I'd never seen before: An invitation. It wasn't a physical invitation or something I could see. It was something I could smell, my sixth sense. She wasn't looking to circumvent the powers that be like I was. She wasn't looking for a way to bypass The Forlorn Order, she was preparing to march up to the front gates, to ring the bell. Because they wanted her. I could feel it.

And she was close.

I sometimes regret telling her about the stealth paint, the "Don't-look-At-Me" technology, that morning at the diner. I didn't expect her to find anything right away. Hell, I wasn't sure I believed it, if I'm being honest. It's just one of those things you hear, something I'd read on the Internet. God knows how many hours I'd wasted doing my own research, looking for blurred lines, cracks in the paint, inconsistencies in wallpaper. It's mind-numbing. But I felt like I needed to prove myself to her, prove that I had something valuable to offer her. I was afraid I'd never get another chance to sit down with her. I saw the earpiece she was wearing. I realized we were being monitored. I don't know if I made the right decisions. Because immediately after that, she disappeared.

I trailed her to The Stratosphere that day, after our breakfast, through the rain. Poor thing. Part of me wanted to say fuck it all. Call the cops and have her picked up. At least then she'd get the medical attention she clearly needed. She'd do her time and have a real shot at life. Whatever business she had with The Forlorn Order had to be nefarious. "I can save her," I told myself. But I didn't call the cops. How could I? Stand in the way of someone so fiercely committed? Sacrilegious!

I watched her go inside the towering casino, through the revolving doors that lead to the main floor, past security guards who looked her up and down but didn't stop her. And she never came out. I waited for hours, only leaving once to track down the Track-Suit Man for my twice-daily dose of "vitamins". We all have our vices in Vegas. But I waited for hours, until after dark. And then I scoured the casino floor for her and couldn't find a trace.

"I'll be damned," I muttered to myself. "She fucking made it."

It was confirmation of what I'd been told, what I'd heard, whispered on dark streets and in the tunnels. There's a network controlled by The Forlorn Order, a "Web" uniting desperate colonies. It would be necessary to transverse this system, I realized, to have any hope of reaching truly undiscovered territories, the ones I'd set my sights on. Past the web, past the feral colonies and displaced societies, past the supposedly impenetrable corridors of Wonderland, past everything anyone has ever dreamed. I'll need to plan accordingly, choose my allies, stockpile my supplies.

I might have spun my wheels for years or given up completely if it wasn't for Sybil, who showed me that The Stratosphere is an important point of penetration. I'll never be able to thank her enough for steadying my course. But at what cost? Because I still think about Sybil, more than I should. A lot. I held vigil outside The Stratosphere for days. I burned a torch in the form of countless cigarettes, chain-smoked, hoping to see her pretty little head pop out, undaunted and unscathed. I even checked hospitals and shelters in the area. I asked around at "The Hole". But she was gone.

I got in touch with her mother, Teresa Evensen-Laghari. She misses her daughter, obviously. I told her my name was Vincent Bugliosi, a highly-motivated rookie cop who had been assigned to her daughter's case. I asked her if there was anything she could tell me about "Darcy" that could help me understand her frame of mind, aspects of her life that might give me the insights necessary to make a breakthrough.

She told me her daughter had Exploding Head Syndrome. I

shit you not, it's a real fucking disease. Sufferers experience insanely loud audio hallucinations, either right when they're falling asleep or right when they're waking up. It's a highly disruptive, terrifying affliction, that some people describe as a giant blast of thunder going off inside their skull. Jesus fucking Christ!

As if this wasn't strange and sad enough, Darcy was diagnosed with something called trigeminal neuralgia or Fothergill Disease, in her early twenties. To say that it causes severe migraines is an understatement. It causes clusters that are so intense, sufferers say it feels like being struck by lightning in the face. Trigeminal neuralgia is probably better known by its Internet name: The Suicide Disease. It's not a joke. There's no cure and sufferers often do attempt to end their lives in order to escape the unbearable pain. Some doctors believe trigeminal neuralgia is the single most painful thing a human can suffer. The average age on onset is sixty, making Darcy's age at diagnosis especially tragic.

Poor Sybil. A head full of thunder and lightning.

"She tried to make a game out of it," her mother told me. I recorded the conversation:

"She imagined that she was kind of a hero or an angel, and her power was enduring pain. I'd hear her thrashing around, but if I tried to help, she'd say, 'Don't touch me! I have to prove to them that I can handle it! I have to prove that I can take it!' Oh, it was so sad. [Long pause] When she'd recover, I'd say, 'Sweetheart, who are "They,"?' And she'd say, 'No one, Mom. It's just how I get through it. She talked about absorbing the pain and harnessing the pain. As a mother, it just breaks your heart."

The rest was basically run of the mill. Drops out of college. Sex and drugs. Car accidents. Obsession with horror movies and dark, occult fiction. "Really disgusting stuff," her mother assured me. Of course there was the incident with the writer, but

Assault with a Deadly Weapon charges were eventually downgraded to Destructive Mayhem. It had been a turning point, her mother told me, and she seemed to be getting her life back on track, adjusting to a regime of Wellbutrin, Lexapro, and Klonopin. No major red flags immediately preceding the stabbing.

And nothing that suggested anywhere new to look beyond the walls of The Stratosphere.

"Promise me you'll find her, Detective Bugliosi," her mother wept. "And when you do, tell her how much I love her."

Jesus Christ, I felt like shit.

Wasn't long after Sybil disappeared that I moved down to the tunnels, permanently. Most people already know that there's a system of storm drains and tunnels built beneath the Las Vegas Strip to protect casinos in the event of flash flooding. Because it happens more often than you think. Now I want to stress, because people make this mistake all the time: These are not cesspools. These aren't disgusting, slimy, putrid sewers like in that fucking ***IT*** movie. These are wide, high, concrete channels. On a hot day, the temperature can be fifteen degrees cooler down here. If you can hold your own, it's really not that much worse than The Whole-Year. Until the inevitable floods come, of course. Those will keep you on your toes.

Been down here months now, probably longer. Biding my time, connecting my dots. Doing my research, stockpiling my supplies. Looking for cracks in the system, secret passageways, clandestine allies. Just waiting for the right time, for all of the stars to align.

And I've taken a scrub under my wing. A new guy. He's pretty green. Doesn't seem to have a lot of ambition. Definitely battling some demons. But I see potential in him. A distant twinkle in his eye, like the soul of an explorer waiting to emerge. Maybe I can mold him into my perfect collaborator. More than that. A consummate companion willing to forge headlong into bottomless pits. Someone like Sybil. Because I'm just not sure I'll ever be able to do it on my own.

As for Sybil, I don't think I'll ever close the "case file" so to speak. I'll never stop looking and keeping my ears to the ground, both on the streets and below them. Maybe we'll cross paths again someday. I certainly hope we will.

I can't help but think of her every time I walk by The Stratosphere. I was over there earlier today, in fact. I smiled because I realized, for the first time, that the Space Needle design kind of looks like a huge syringe of heroin, pointing straight into the ground. I smiled when I imagined all that heroin, coursing beneath the city, collecting into rivers, streaming through the storm drains. I smiled imagining me and Sonny, just dipping our needles straight into this warm amber flow, filling our veins with it until we reach a stage of ultimate bliss.

Absolute warm oblivion.

About the Author

Photo credit: Ama Lea

Over the past decade-plus, Joshua Millican has proven himself to be a horror expert of the highest caliber. After establishing a personal blog in 2011, Millican quickly became one of the horror genre's premiere journalists, contributing to many websites before ultimately landing at Dread Central in 2016. One of the top horror outlets on the planet, Millican served as Editor-in-Chief from 2019 through 2021. In addition to writing, Millican has been a member of numerous festival juries, a popular podcast guest, and has even scored a handful of acting gigs. His talk show *Chronic Horror* (sidelined by the Pandemic) explored the intersection of horror movie fandom and cannabis culture. Now married and a father for the first time, Millican is excited to pen more hardcore horror/sci-fi/fantasy fiction for Encyclopocalypse Publications.

Follow Joshua Millican on Twitter at @josh_millican.

CPSIA information can be obtained
at www.ICGtesting.com
Printed in the USA
SHW031004070623
58JS00005B/201